Lamplight on the Hearth

Miriam's Journal

A Fruitful Vine
A Winding Path
A Joyous Heart
A Treasured Friendship
A Golden Sunbeam

Joy's Journal

Tall Cedars Homestead
Beechwood Acres
Majestic Oak Memoirs
Forget-Me-Not Lane
Lamplight on the Hearth

Miriam Joy, who now goes by the name Joy, was just a little girl in the "Miriam's Journal series." In Joy's Journal, she marries Kermit, moves first to Tall Cedars Homestead, then to Beechwood Acres, reminisces in Majestic Oak Memoirs and Forget-Me-Not Lane, and now lights up her hearth in Montana.

Joy's Journal #5

Lamplight on the Hearth

Carrie Bender

Masthof Press
219 Mill Road
Morgantown, PA 19543-9516

Published 2005
Masthof Press
219 Mill Road
Morgantown, PA 19543-9516

This story is fiction.
Parts are based on actual happenings,
but not always in the correct time
they occurred.

Contents

Part One

Back to Montana

We finally arrived at the Swift River community yesterday, just in time for the spring calving season on our farm. It was a busy, busy day, but with the help of our neighbors and our *"maud and gnecht,"* Treva and Jared, by evening everything was in place.

I like the layout of this house—there's a little room just the right size for Hannah beside ours upstairs, and there's even a play-room downstairs where Hannah and Henry can play when he's a little older. There's a wide front hall extending from the front to the back, that seems to divide the house in half. The large down-stairs room that we'll use for our parlor has a big fireplace and mantle, and a built-in china closet. There's even an office for Kermit, where we put his desk and file cabinet. The previous owners left several big, round braided rugs, which I'm really thank-ful for, as they're not very old and give the house a warm, homey touch. The best part of it, though, is the huge bay window over-looking the Swift River Valley, the river itself, and the pine moun-tains beyond.

It was a good thing we arrived when we did, because by evening a fresh snowfall had started and kept up all night. This morning everything was drifted shut, with mounds and swirls of beautiful snow covering all the landscape. Kermit was glad for Jared's help in shoveling a path to the barn, cattle sheds, and other outbuildings.

Treva is at the sewing machine, making new curtains for her bedroom, and I'm spending a little more time with the chil-dren, as they didn't get much attention from me yesterday. I'm sure that we'll be able to make ourselves at home here, and we'll be able to find plenty to do to keep us busy.

Verse for today:

> *Give us a calm, a thankful heart,*
> *From every murmur free;*
> *The blessing of Thy grace impart,*
> *And make us live to Thee.*

March 2

After being away from it so long, we marvel anew at the awesome majesty of our surroundings—the tall pine trees etched against the mountains, the enormous blue sky above, and the scenic, frozen river winding its way through the valley. Tonight I went along out to help feed the cattle, and took some time to gaze up into the dazzling, star-studded expanse above. In Montana, the stars seem so very bright, clear, and close—positively awesome. I heard the coyotes serenading the moonlit evening from far off in the hills and suddenly shivered, and hurried into the warmth and safety of the barn. It will take some getting used to again . The echoes of the north and also the silences. No wonder Kermit wanted to come back, for it's home to him, and I'm sure that it will be just as dear to me after awhile.

This forenoon Kermit's Mom stopped in to see her grandchildren and our new home. She's a dear and her visit was greatly appreciated. I was making apple dumplings, and she thought they smelled so good while they were baking that she accepted our invitation to stay for dinner. Luckily, I had put a big beef roast in the oven. We also had baked potatoes with cheese sauce and corn. But she liked the dumplings best, and even asked for the recipe. I got the recipe from Mom, and so I call them:

Mamma's Apple Dumplings

2 cups flour	2 tablespoons sugar
2 teaspoons baking powder	a pinch of salt
1/3 cup milk	1/3 cup shortening

Mix the above ingredients like pie dough, then divide it into four parts. Peel four apples. Roll out each quarter part of dough into a five-inch circle. Place two halves of an apple in the center and wrap up the dough around it. Place the four dumplings in a three-quart casserole, and pour the following syrup over them (mix together and bring to a boil):

      1 cup water   1/3 cup sugar   1/3 cup butter

Bake at 350 degrees for 50 minutes, or until golden brown. Serve with milk or cream.

There weren't enough dumplings to reach around, so Treva and I shared one, and Mom shared hers with Hannah.

Ya well, it's time to get the children to bed for Kermit's through telling them their bedtime story and their eyelids are drooping. Sweet dreams.

March 3

I wrote a letter tonight, to Estelle, my pen pal from Johnstown. I met her when we had gone to Johnstown, to see the flood museums and the big empty lake bed. We exchanged addresses, and have been corresponding by mail ever since. I'll have to send her my new address, or I won't get anymore letters. She's twenty years older than I am, but seemed to take a real interest in our way of life, and said she'd like to come visit us sometime. I doubt that she'll come this far, though! She's an interesting letter writer, a knowledgeable person, and a dedicated Christian besides. Her great-great-grandmother lived in Johnstown during the time of the big flood, but since their house was on the hillside, it was spared. It would be interesting to hear her account of May 31, 1889, when the big South Fork dam broke. What a tragedy that flood was—leaving over 2,000 dead and 27,000 homeless. It's unfathomable indeed.

Today Baby (Henry) cut his first tooth, so perhaps (hopefully) he will sleep better again. Hannah went along to the barn with Kermit tonight, bundled up in layers and layers, plus a coat and scarves. She loves being out there, and will like it even better when the calves start to arrive, which will be any day now.

Poems for today:
> *My little toddler's chubby hand,*
> *Entwines my heart with love's strong band.*

She gives me her precious gift so sweet—
Could I bring such love to my Master's feet?

That one was for Hannah, and this one's for Henry:

My precious little baby boy;
Oh, what a gift—what a joy!
Eyes a-shining, lovelight aglow;
These sacred moments, who can know?

March 4

Kermit hitched up the two big work horses to the bobsled this afternoon—the ones Pop Mullet sent over. The children were napping, so I quickly bundled up and joined him. There's no sign of spring approaching yet, for this morning it was just under zero degrees again. I try not to think back to Forget-Me-Not Lane and the red-winged blackbirds calling their *kong-a-rees* announcing spring's imminent arrival, and the daffodils and hyacinths pushing up through the moist earth (here they're buried under snowdrifts), or the early robins hopping about and chirping. But one sure sign that spring will be coming soon, will be the arrival of the baby calves. In spite of the hardships and rigors that go with the calving season, I'm looking forward to it. For, in remembering it from our Tall Cedars Homestead days, it's very rewarding, as well as challenging. We'll be glad for Treva and Jared's help.

The sun actually felt a bit warm this afternoon, as it dazzled on the glistening snow and ice. The new horses stepped lively as we headed down the windswept ravine with our load of hay. The cows were huddled together behind the windbreak for shelter and began to stamp around and moo impatiently when they saw us coming.

The sun shone down through the snow-laden pines, making alternating patches of sunshine and blue-white shadows on the snow. Kermit quickly unloaded the hay, and I walked a short way into the woods, looking for princess pine and partridge berries. I startled a big buck out of a thicket, and with a flip of his tail, he went crashing away. Kermit declared he would bring his gun along next time for venison steaks would be a real tasty variation from beef for a change.

I found some nice red berries, and Kermit, with eyes a-twinkle, took them from me and twined them over my shoulder and scarf, and standing back to appraise the picture, whistled in admiration and said I'd pass for a Snow Queen. He's still the same charming, lovable guy! I teasingly stooped to pack a snowball, but a movement at the edge of the clearing stopped me. It was a bold, yet wary coyote, peering around a pile of rocks. His gray fur was standing on end and he watched us with gleaming, baleful eyes. I sprang up on the sled then, and Kermit again resolved not to come back there again without his gun. I think the coyote was smart enough to know he didn't have a gun or he wouldn't have been so bold. The wily creature merely slunk away out of sight into a crevice in the rock. The very rock he will probably be on tonight to lift his muzzle to the moon, to fill the Swift River Valley with his eerie, spine-tingling howls which will echo crazily back from the mountains across the river. It makes you think of the wild, rugged west, in the pioneer days!

Ya well, Hannah has her favorite books, *A Child's Garden of Verses* and the big bedtime storybook, and is asking for a story before it's nitey-nite time. Baby has just had his bath and is in his pajamas, and Kermit's teaching him to "pat-a-cake."

Verse for today:
> *Love the moments that are tender;*
> *Lift your heart in thankful song—*
> *Love the precious, golden moments—*
> *Babyhood will not last long.*

March 5

We had a visit from Chuck, our farmhand at Tall Cedars Homestead. He was familiar with this area when he was a boy, and so, had some interesting things to tell us about the neighborhood and this farm. I kept the coffee pot filled and put a plate full of doughnuts on the table, and he kept us royally entertained. He said that the big hill just north of the cattle ravine used to be called Rosebriar Hill years ago.

While he was here a carriage drove in. It was Mom and Pop Mullet, so they got to visit with Chuck, too. They were interested, too, in hearing about this farm of years ago, and Pop remembered that mention was made of Rosebriar Hill on the deed. Chuck had quite a few interesting stories to tell, and then he stated his purpose for coming—he'd like to have a job as farmhand with us on this farm. He offered to work for his room and board, saying that he's not as young as he used to be, but that his experience with the cows and calves might come in handy. Pop and Kermit thought so, too, and his offer was accepted. So, plans are now, that we'll be getting the second floor of the carriage shed ready for him to move into. He prefers that to moving right in with us, even though there would be plenty of room in our big house. He won't be bringing his TV set either, for he says there's not much more than trash on it these days. He has a guitar though, and asked politely if we'd mind his playing it in the evenings after the work is done. His crinkly-twinkly eyed smile deepened when Kermit told him he has no objections.

On Monday he and Kermit plan to paint the walls of his living quarters and I will make curtains for the windows. It should be a cozy home after it's finished, with a view over the Swift River Valley. He said he will be able to make himself at home anywhere his coffee pot is, and his old woodstove to keep him warm. He stayed for supper and we found out that he did have a wife years ago. Her name was Maggie. They were married only two years when she died, which was over 40 years ago. I wondered what she died from, but he was wiping away years when he told us about her, so I didn't ask. He never remarried and so never had much of a family life.

After he had left and while the children played, Kermit and I sat talking about all he had told us about this farm. We're anxious to explore Rosebriar Hill after the snow melts, especially in June, when the wild roses will be blooming. I had been hoping there would be at least one rosebush on this place, for they are favorites of mine. Kermit said that he will buy me another rosebush on my next birthday, just like the one he bought for me at each place we lived. This is the fourth place we're living at and if we'd have them all together, we'd have a little rose garden.

It's time for the bedtime stories, but Hannah is still happily arranging her tea set on the little table Kermit made for her and Henry is playing with his blocks. We'll enjoy these quiet evenings before the hectic calving season arrives.

Verse for today:

Through briars, thorns, and brambles,
Christ seeks with anxious heart;
O'er mountain vale, or forest wild, or in the crowded mart,
O'er ocean main, o'er desert sands,
He seeks the wide world o'er.

In gilded palace of the rich, in cottage of the poor.
He seeks His wandering sheep to bring them to the fold.

Who can describe the howling of the coyotes echoing down from the hills? Chuck says it's like a prolonged howl which the coyote lets out, then runs after it, and bites it into small pieces. An apt description indeed. Tonight they're really serenading us —maybe they feel it in their bones that spring can't be far away.

We attended church services yesterday, and it was good to fellowship with the people here in the Swift River District. The sleigh ride was delightful, too, flying through the frosty air, with the children tucked snugly under the blankets, and seeing the snow-covered countryside whizzing by.

Kermit had some exciting news for me this morning—we have some closer neighbors than we thought we did! While bringing back a stray cow that had wandered up Rosebriar Hill, he discovered a little house on the other side of the hill nestled in among the trees. It looked neat and well-kept, so I'm hoping they'll be of the "race that knows Joseph" (kindred spirits, as Anne of Green Gables would say). I wish Kermit would find time to repair my snowshoes, for I'd love to walk back there some sunny afternoon, while Treva babysits. It's kind of easy to get "cabin fever" this time of year, before the excitement of the calving season begins.

This afternoon I finished the curtains I was making for Chuck's windows. I took them out to his living quarters above the carriage house and put them up and did some other finishing touches. The paint that Kermit and Chuck put on the walls this forenoon must have been the fast-drying kind, and already, this afternoon, Chuck was bringing his things over and they were putting them in place. Oh, yes, I forgot to mention the piece of blue-checkered linoleum they laid down as soon as the paint was dry. I couldn't believe how fast it all came about, and how nice it looked when the blue-flowered curtains were at the windows. After the furniture was in, I helped to unpack his boxes of belongings. What fun it was adding the homey touches—a throw rug in front of the sofa, a picture at just the right spot on the wall, a bouquet of dried flowers on the middle of the table, and a furry-looking throw with a picture of a deer on it for the armchair.

When Chuck left to get some things he needed at the hardware store, Kermit came in to see if I wanted to go along back to the ravine with some medication for a cow in the shed back there. I did, and it was an exhilarating excursion, riding double with him on horseback, through the crisp, cold air. I'm glad for Kermit's sake, that we are out here, doing the things he loves in the big outdoors, rather than back near Forget-Me-Not Lane, and him working in the "stuffy" woodworking shop which he never really learned to like. I'll have to write to Aunt Miriam sometime and thank her for the advice.

I had a very welcome letter from friend Sadie today, bringing us the latest news from the "old neighborhood," and bringing us up-to-date on all that has happened since we left. She had enclosed a poem which I really liked, so I'll copy it here:

> *I dare not dwell on past failures,*
> *That Christ, through His blood has erased;*
> *I dare not, 'twould make my hands weaker,*
> *The battle before must be faced.*
> *I dare not dwell on my weakness,*
> *For that leaves discouragement in.*
> *For I will go forward in Jesus,*
> *And trust Him to cleanse me from sin.*
> *- Author Unknown*

March 8

I made Mom Mullet's chicken recipe tonight for supper and received "rave reviews," so I'll copy it here:

Golden Chicken Bake

2 fryers, cut up
1 1/2 cups flour
1/2 cup grated Parmesan
   cheese
1 1/2 teaspoons poultry
   seasoning
2 teaspoons paprika

2 teaspoons seasoned salt
1/2 teaspoon black pepper
2 teaspoons regular salt
1/2 cup butter
1 egg, beaten
1/2 cup water

Mix dry ingredients (including cheese) in a large plastic bag. Mix egg and water. Dip chicken in egg mixture, then in flour mixture.

Place pieces in single layer in baking pan in which the butter has been melted. Bake at 400 degrees for one-half hour, then turn the chicken and reduce heat to 350 degrees and bake for another one-half hour, or until tender and golden.

Chuck was here for supper and he declared it was the best he'd ever eaten.

He told us some more stories of his boyhood days in the wilds of Canada. When he was 12 years old, his parents hitched their two horses to the wagon, and with his little sister, went to the nearest town 15 miles away, for supplies. They stayed at a friend's house for the night, so he was home alone to feed the stock and keep the fire burning. After supper he was lying on the rug in front of the fireplace, looking at a magazine, when he heard a disturbance and a stamping around in the stable, which was not far from the house. He quickly lit a lantern, grabbed a gun, and went to investigate. It was pitch dark by then and his hair stood on end as he headed for the stable. He felt sure that somewhere outside the circle of his lantern light, there was a big beast hiding in the shadows—either a mountain lion or a bear. Fearfully, he made his way to the stable, half expecting something to leap out at him anytime.

The horse and cow in the stable had calmed down somewhat by then, so he locked the stable door, hung the lantern on a hook and fed the stock. He still felt uneasy as he got the pail and milking stool to milk the cow, but by then the animals seemed to have forgotten about whatever had frightened them, and were eating their grain and hay as if nothing had happened. After the chores were done, he took the gun and lantern and tramped around a bit outside, but whatever had been there must have left, for all seemed quiet and peaceful. Nevertheless, he kept his loaded gun by the door that evening, and didn't rest easy, for he knew that the beast could come back anytime. He was scared and wished his parents would be home, but after awhile he decided to go to bed. He hadn't been sleeping long, when he was awakened by the horse's terrified neighs and a terrible ruckus in the stable. By the time he had the lantern lit and was heading for the barn, he was too late, for he saw a big bear leaving the stable and heading for the woods. He fired shots after it, but the bear kept on going, darting off into the night.

Chuck was glad the bear had been frightened off, but dreaded going into the stable to see what had happened. He said his heart sank to his toes when he saw that the horse had been killed! He had raking claw marks down over his rump, but they later figured he had been killed by breaking his neck from his terrified thrashing around. The cow was unhurt and the bear didn't come back, but Chuck had a night of awful anxiety standing guard at the stable door. The next day the neighbor men tracked down the bear (whose tracks were bigger than a man's hand) and killed it. The bear had some bullet wounds from the evening before, so Chuck must've hit him, though not at the right place.

Oh dear, I hope the wild beasts have all gone far away from Rosebriar Hill, but I do know that they can travel far in a night. When calving season comes, we must be on the lookout for them.

Verse for today:
So we Thy people and sheep of Thy pasture will
give Thee thanks forever: We will shew forth
Thy praise to all generations. (Psalm 79:13)

March 9

Snow, snow, and more snow! Deep, deep drifts, with mounds and swirls sculpted by the wind, cover everything. It's beautiful, and yet, our hearts turn to thoughts of springtime, when the singing birds, and fragrant warm breezes return. Until then, I'll enjoy being "cooped up" with my little ones! Hannah is becoming a "mother's little helper." She helps to fold the laundry, and wants her own rag to help when I wash the windows and furniture. She'd even grab a paring knife to help peel potatoes if I'd let her. It reminds me of the verse:

From scrubbing the floor to shining the windows,
To setting the dinner table;
Most children like to be helpful,
Until they're old enough to be able!

Henry is walking along the furniture now and crawling everywhere. They're both the sunshine of our home, a blessing indeed, and we're hoping for a dozen. Large families have more fun together and no matter how many children in a family there's always enough love for them all. In fact, love can be multiplied, as it says in this poem:

> *When George was a baby upon my knee*
> *I wondered if I could love another as he.*
> *Maydene was added, and then there were two,*
> *Love wasn't divided, love just grew.*
> *Then when wee Charlie came along,*
> *My love for him was just as strong.*
> *When Perry and Merry joined our group,*
> *My mother love took a loop-de-loop.*
> *Love didn't subtract; love didn't divide;*
> *God's gift of love just multiplied!*
>
> *- Author Unknown*

Being a mother has its hectic moments, though, like tonight when Hannah spilled a pitcher of milk and it splashed all over the kitchen floor. Before I could stop him, Henry came crawling and slipped into the middle of the puddle with a splash. I was cooking a kettle full of caramel pudding on the stove, which I plum forgot about in all of the commotion, The next thing I smelled was the pudding scorched to the bottom of the kettle. Just then Chuck walked in the door, took one look at the situation, and retreated in a hurry, probably glad that he has peace and quiet at his place.

The children are in bed now, so I'll take the time to copy this poem, which is a reminder to be patient with the childen's childish prattle and questions:

Evening Muse

> *Today I was fraught with the cares of life,*
> *As I hurried my tasks all the whil,e*
> *And had no time to talk with my child.*
> *But I brushed him out of my way,*
> *And I spoke harsh words,*
> *When he hindered my task,*
> *Or paused by my side to ask:*

March 10

Today we finally had some sunshine, although there were a few big, lazy flakes drifting down, adding more beauty to the picturesque countryside. Kermit repaired my snowshoes, and I happily donned them and bundled up to brave the elements, intending to find out who lives in the little house over on the other side of Rosebriar Hill. As I traipsed down the wooded road, the mountains in the distance seemed more wild, rugged, and awesome than ever. The picture of untamed beauty! The sun dazzled on the snowy peaks, lighting them up with a glorious splendor, and once again, I was reminded of the words in the song, "How Great Thou Art." Even the gentle wooded slopes were majestic today, for the stately trees, (mostly pines, cedars, and spruce) were covered with sparkling caps of snow—the branches laden down with it. The air was crisp, cold, and exhilarating as I made my way along the trail between the gigantic pine trees, reaching like sentinels up into the big blue sky. It was a splendid walk and I didn't even see any bold coyotes slinking away into the shadows behind a rock. The chickadees were flitting around in the bushes, perky as ever, with their little black caps and cheeky tunes, and a bright flash of red in a treetop told me that our pair of cardinals were back. As I passed by the ravine, the cows eyed me curiously and mooed softly as I passed, and I wondered if they knew that they would soon be proud protective mammas. On the other side of Rosebriar Hill, I found the little house nestled among the trees. I stopped to marvel at the magnificent view they have from there, then removed my snowshoes and headed up the walkway, which had been neatly cleared of snow. But, much to my disappointment, no one seemed to be at home, so I'll have to wait until some other time to make their acquaintance.

On the way back, I spotted a cow that appeared to be showing signs of calving. I told Kermit, and he and Chuck are back there now, getting her up to the barn. It's time to keep close watch on the cows from now on.

On the way in I got the mail, and found a fat pack from Mom and all the rest back home. *Wunderbaar!* They're still busy caring for dear babies whose mothers are in prison, and loving every minutes of it, as Mom wrote. They miss us though, and are longing to see us again, just as we are to see them.

Mom sent a noodle recipe for just a small batch, which is excellent for me, for I didn't get myself a noodle-making machine yet. Here it is:

Homemade Noodle Dough

2 1/4 to 2 1/2 cups flour	1 tablespoon oil
2 eggs	1 teaspoon salt
1 egg yolk	1/3 cup water

Combine the eggs, oil, salt, and water, and beat with a wire wisk. Add the flour, mix into a dough, and knead until pliable. Let rest 30 minutes, then roll out the dough and cut into one-fourth inch strips with a pizza cutter. Cook in boiling water for 7 minutes and top with browned butter, if desired. Season to taste.

I already tried the recipe . We had it for supper and it was as good as the "Little Spatzlein" I like to make sometimes, which are similar.

And here's a poem which I found in an old hand-copied poem book, in honor of Mom who did her best to teach me to cook:

Mamma's Recipes

Mamma's the finest cook on earth.
She told me long ago,
Bread's no good unless you add,
Some loving to the dough.
And when you're baking pies, she said,
"A pinch of faith and trust,
If added to the shortening,
Makes a flaky, tender crust."
Compassion by the spoonful,
In the batter of a cake,
Makes it come out light and fluffy,
And the finest you can make.
Now these things cannot be purchased,
In the store across the way,
But Mamma keeps them in her heart,
And uses them each day.

- Author Unknown

I might as well copy the "Little Spatzlein" recipe too, which I got from Aunt Miriam. It really is good topped with plenty of brown butter, too.

Spatzlein (Little Sparrows)

1 egg	2 quarts boiling water
1 cup water	1 1/2 teaspoons salt
2 1/2 cups flour	

Beat egg thoroughly. Add water and beat until well blended with egg. Add flour and beat until smooth. Bring salt water to a boil and drop spatzlein into water. To do this, tilt bowl containing batter in a position that it can be cut with the edge of a spoon as it pours over the edge of the bowl. The spatzlein should be an inch long and one-fourth inch in diameter. Cook for three minutes af-

ter batter is all in the water. Drain in colander and top with browned butter. Makes 6 servings.

Time to go, for the Mullets are coming tonight. Pop wants to help get the shed ready out back of the barn, for an extra maternity pen for the cows. If any of the cows are calving he's even going to stay here for the night, and Mom's going to take the rig home alone. After Pop has his fill of the calving excitement, Chuck will take him home.

March 11

The first Hereford calf arrived last night and Kermit was jubilant. Pop Mullet is in on the excitement of calving time, too, for the cows and calves belong to him. Kermit has more experience than he does, but neither of them are as experienced as Chuck. Pop is going to stay to help for a few days. Early this morning, Kermit and I took our turn to watch the cows and it was almost an exact repeat of the calving time at Tall Cedars Homestead—every twig and bush beautifully frosted white with hoarfrost in the below zero fog, and a silvery moon low on the horizon. We were thankful there was no wind, for it's a mighty cold world for the babies to be ushered into, when it's below zero and windy. We found three Herefords showing signs of calving, and by the time we had the last one in the birthing pen, the second calf had arrived— a strapping bull calf, bawling lustily, and soon nuzzling for nourishment. I'm afraid there will be nary a dull moment these next several weeks, for the cows will have to be watched day and night, and it could even get to be quite hectic. But it's a rewarding sight to see the dozens of little calves who are vigorously healthy and growing, with their mamas. I hope there won't be any hungry bears or cougars coming down from the mountains in search of a tender veal meal.

Treva's making Southern pies. It's her Dad's favorite kind, and so I'll copy the recipe here:

3/4 cup grape-nuts cereal	3/4 cup sugar
1/2 cup warm water	1 cup King syrup,
3 eggs, well beaten	no molasses

3 tablespoons melted butter   1 unbaked pie crust
1 teaspoon vanilla   prepared whipped cream
1/8 teaspoon salt

Combine cereal and water; let stand until water is absorbed. Meanwhile, blend eggs with sugar, add syrup, butter, vanilla, and salt. Fold in softened cereal. Pour into pie shell and bake at 350 degrees for 50 minutes, or until filling is puffed completely across the top. Cool. Garnish with whipped cream. Sprinkle with additional cereal, if desired.

Kermit, Jared, and Pop Mullet are still outside with the cows, so I'll make a pot of hot chocolate to help warm them up when they come in.

Verse for today:
> *Love consecrates the humblest act,*
> *And sanctifies each deed,*
> *It sheds a benediction sweet,*
> *And hallows every need.*

March 12

Hannah is all excited about what's in the big box behind the woodstove—it's a little newborn calf! Chuck found it half frozen out in the ravine, born before the mamma cow could be put into the maternity pen. He wrapped it in his big coat and carried it into the house, thawed it out in warm water in the tub, then rubbed it down with old rags until it seemed to revive. Last, he wrapped it in an old blanket with a hot water bottle tucked in. I've been feeding it (or rather, him) clostrom milk in a bottle, and he seems to be getting perkier every hour. In fact, he became so lively awhile ago, that he upset the box and walked out into the middle of the kitchen floor on wobbly, unsteady legs, looking as cute and inquisitive as could be. Hannah thought it was great fun, and even Henry laughed out loud and clapped his hands. Treva says it's high time that calf gets taken out to its mamma, where it belongs. She's kneading bread dough and wants to make a pan of cinnamon buns with a portion of the dough. Later she will take her turn helping

out in the calf barn. Jared (our former hired boy) has another job now, since we have Chuck's experienced help, we can make out without him.

We'll have to watch out for bears after the calves are out on the range. They're mighty lean and hungry when they come out of hibernation in the spring, and will travel far for delicacies such as choice, tender veal—the helpless newborn calves.

Verse for today:
If aught good thou canst not say,
Of thy brother, foe or friend,
Take thou, then, the silent way,
Lest in word thou shouldst offend.
- Anon.

April 10

I see that nearly a month has passed since my last journal entry and now we are into the beauties of springtime. Rivulets of water are running down off Rosebriar Hill, through crevices and gullies among the rocks. The air is fragrant with the scent of moist earth and of green things poking through. The hillside is dotted with Hereford cows and their offspring playfully gambol about them.

I went for a walk this afternoon, back around Rosebriar Hill and stopped at the little house back there, but no one was home this time either. Oh well, at least I had a delightful walk, and the view back there is breathtaking with the backdrop of stately, majestic trees and mountains in the distance. It's just the spot I'd pick for my *"daudyhaus"* (grandparents' house) if I were the Mullets. In the meadow the grass was greener already, and I found a few shy wild violets. Soon there will be dancing buttercups and lacy green ferns bordering the woods path. The calves were cavorting happily around their grazing mammas, and I could hardly believe how they'd grown already.

Golden Gem for today:
Don't be discouraged because of your past
failures and ever-present imperfections,
rather always rise up bravely after a fall, ask
for and accept God's forgiveness, ready for
a new beginning, striving afresh to crucify
self and its whims and to continually abide in
Christ.

We had special visitors tonight—Mr. and Mrs. Simmons, and Emily, the little girl we used to babysit and her little brother, Ethan. That was very much appreciated, for we hadn't seen them for a long time. They still have Mini, their pet ferret, and he is still in excellent health. They weren't here long when another car drove in, and it was Mrs. Bryan and Bethany! They had this all planned to surprise us, bringing cake and ice cream for us! It seemed like the old days at Tall Cedars Homestead, bringing back precious memories.

We walked partways back to Rosebriar Hill since it was such a beautiful evening with the mountains seeming so close. The full moon was rising up over the top in the darkening sky. The coyotes were howling from the far-off hills and a great-horned owl called from the pine tree.

When we got back, Emily and Hannah had a little tea party on the porch while the grown-ups sat and visited. It would be fun to have Emily here everyday again, because it is such good entertainment for Hannah. Bethany served the cake and ice cream out on the porch and we stayed until it got too chilly for Henry. It was such an enjoyable evening, another one for our chest of precious memories.

Golden Gem for today:
To pray is to act toward God as the child does to its mother, the poor man towards the rich, eager to do him good, the friend toward his friend, who longs to show him affection.

April 12

With the coming of spring and the melting of the snow, hopefully we'll be able to explore some more of our farm and neighborhood. The hillsides will soon be greening up—growing more grass for the cows and their frisky calves, and the woods will be ringing with the joyous song of the birds. Already the air is warmer and more balmy, and also fragrant with the scent newly-grown plants and moist soil. Out back of the barn I found a little rivulet of water rushing down from the mountain, gurgling over rocks and miniature falls, and emptying into the Swift River. I suppose later it will dry up, but for now it's very picturesque.

Friends Rachal and Ben spent the day here. Ben helped Kermit with the branding and Rachal and I made noodles, while Treva watched the little ones. It seemed like old times again. Rachal's such a jolly and cheerful person, and such an inspiration to me. Her two little boys are robust, cherubic, and into everything, and with our two helping, they were quite a set. Treva truly had her hands full.

In today's mail I received a letter from Estelle, my pen pal from Johnstown. She wrote that the city of Johnstown was founded by, and named after, an Amishman—Joseph Johns or Joseph Schantz (in Dutch). That was news to me, but Rachal knew all about it. In fact, Joseph was even a distant relative of hers, a great-great-great-great -uncle, or something like that. She'd love to see the flood museum sometime, too, as she read about the 1889 Johnstown flood in a book. But she said it isn't very likely she will ever see it, for if and when they ever do get to Pennsylvania, she will have a lot of friends and relatives to visit and time will be short.

Today was one of those especially meaningful days, that will furnish material for our memory chest of golden hours. I'll take the time to copy a fitting verse on friendship:

> *Still hand in hand, our journey through;*
> *As pilgrims may we go.*
> *Mingling our joys as helpers true;*
> *And sharing every woe.*

May 16

On Ascension Day we packed a picnic lunch and headed for the hills and woods, to explore some more of our surroundings. Everywhere we looked the earth was vibrant with the beauties of springtime—the lush green grasses and shy wildflowers, the birds singing with joyful abandon, the majestic pines and mountains, the big, blue sky overhead—all so unbearably awesome and breathtaking. We saw a flash of blue in the treetops and wondered if it could have been an indigo bunting. We heard pine siskins, wood pewees, and thrushes, and many others whose notes I couldn't identify.

Chuck and Treva carried the picnic lunch while we hiked down to the river. We put Baby in the back carrier and Hannah toddled along, exclaiming delightfully about the bunnies we chased from their hiding places, and the squirrels chattering from the branches overhead. She just had her second birthday, so Treva made her a cake with two candles for her to blow out and Mom sent a card and gift.

We've been so busy this spring that it seems I haven't had much time for journal writing. We haven't even gotten around to meeting our new neighbors yet, few and far between as they are.

We passed the small house up in the woods on the other side of Rosebriar Hill. It is surrounded by pines and a rocky canyon to the left of it. I tried to visit several times to find out what the occupants are like, but there was never anyone home. We stopped in again on our Ascension Day hike, but again, no one was home. It looked neat and homey, as though someone lived there who cared for it lovingly. There was a low, rock wall all around it, with interesting looking beds of ferns and irises and a little rock wishing well, spilling over with petunias.

A small stream flowed out of the woods behind the place, and trickled down over an opening in the rock wall, and flowed between winding banks through the yard. A quaint little wooden bridge spanned the brook, and a bed of wildflowers and ferns gave it a wild, woodsy look. I found myself wishing that Sadie could buy that house and live there, but who knows, maybe the lady that lives there is just as good-natured and friendly as Sadie.

It has to be a woman, for it has a woman's touch according to the looks of the place. Time to go, for Hannah's ready with her bedtime books, and Kermit's still busy outside and won't have time for her bedtime stories tonight.

Happy Golden Ramblings

Happiness is . . .

> . . . having 25 quarts of canned strawberry jam on the counter.
>
> . . . discovering a rambling rose bush, covered with hundreds of shy, pink roses, cascading down over a rocky ledge in the meadow
>
> . . . having Kermit's foot heal as good as new, without any infection, after one of the big workhorses stepped on his bare foot
>
> . . . getting letters from my family "back home"
>
> . . . having both children in good health again after being miserable with chicken pox
>
> . . . Kermit's Mom arriving in time for supper, with two big, store-bought pizzas
>
> . . . having the bills all paid, at last
>
> . . . having a nice garden, adequate rainfall, and the weeds under control
>
> . . . sitting on the rocker, holding both Hannah and Henry, and counting my blessings
>
> . . . knowing that Kermit is happy in doing the kind of work he loves

Mom and Pop Mullet stopped in tonight for a few minutes on the way back from a sale. I told Mom about the lovely roses in the meadow that are too lovely to be wild ones, and she had an explanation for it. The former owner's wife had a beloved pet dog, her constant companion for nearly 15 years, and when he died, she buried him there. She planted the rose bush on the spot as a "memorial" for him, and afterward spent a good deal of time down there, sitting on a rock, reminiscing about her pet. How lovely, at least if she hadn't any children and her husband didn't mind.

I'm so glad the children are over their chicken pox at last. I think I might have stayed home from church at Swift River that Sunday, had I known they'd be exposed. Oh well, it's over now, and hopefully they won't get it again.

Verse for today:
> *We know that scenes, not always bright,*
> *Must unto us be given;*
> *But over all give Thou the light,*
> *Of love, and truth, and Heaven.*

July 27

I went berrying this afternoon, while the children napped and Treva worked on her quilt patch, a friendship quilt for a friend of hers that has mononucleosis.

I was up on the hillside slipping through the brambles intent on finding the plumpest and juiciest berries without getting too scratched from the thorns, when I was startled by a surprised face appearing through the opening in the hedge. I quickly dropped back, then went around the hedge to see who was there and came face to face with not one, but two berry pickers. The two introduced themselves as sisters, Helen and Rosalie Wert, who are the owners of the little house in the woods. They looked to be kindred spirits, pleasant and friendly-like and I soon found them to be as good-natured as one could wish. And, what's more, they were old-fashioned and utterly unworldy—a surprising thing in today's day and age.

We were soon chatting away like old friends, and I soon found out why they appeared to be so—they were of German descent, and were also originally from Berks County, Pennsylvania. I'm sure that we shall be good friends from now on, and we both wonder why we didn't get together sooner. I suppose it's understandable, as their long drive winds down, north of the canyon, and comes out on the logging road back there. They're both in their thirties, maiden ladies, pretty and pleasingly plump.

Helen is a nurse in an old people's home, and Rosalie works in a daycare center in Little Falls. I feel like it will be almost as good as having Sadie living there, now that we got to know them.

I invited them over for supper on Sunday evening, and they graciously accepted, promising to bring a salad. That's something to look forward to!

Verse for today:
> *I would love Thee; every blessing,*
> *Flows to me from out Thy throne;*
> *I would love Thee; he who loves Thee,*
> *Never feels himself alone.*

August 5

We hear the whippoorwills calling in the morning and evening, and the weather has turned unusually sultry for this part of the country. Where has the time flown to? Can it really be midsummer already? Almost before we know it, the winds of winter will be upon us again. Oh well, I love winter, too, for there's more time for things like making quilts, sewing, and journal writing.

The Wert sisters did come for supper on Sunday evening, jolly and amiable as I had remembered them, and promptly took to Hannah and Henry, lavishing their love on them in a way that was gratifying to me. Henry was a little shy at first, but they won him over with the gift they brought for him—a stuffed bunny with pink ears. For Hannah they had a Little Golden Book, which Rosalie read aloud to her. When she was through it, Hannah brought them a whole stack of her books to read aloud, and this won her over completely, too. The evening went too fast, but we'll be back and forth regularly now, I'm sure. The salad they brought was delicious, and Helen gave me the recipe, which I'll copy here:

Cauliflower Salad

1 head cauliflower	1 small onion
1 head lettuce	2 hard-boiled eggs

Dressing: 1/4 cup sugar and salt to taste

Topping:

2 cups mayonnaise	1/2 lb. bacon, fried
2 cups grated cheese	and crumbled

Chop up the vegetables in a bowl and toss with the mayonnaise and seasoning. Top with cheese and bacon. Refrigerate for one-half hour before serving. Serves 8.

Helen and Rosalie Wert planned a picnic for us at a scenic spot near the base of Rosebriar Hill. They couldn't have chosen a more delightful day weatherwise, with the golden yellow sunshine all around us and the late-summer wildflowers blooming. They had set up their charcoal grill to make hamburgers and also served home-baked beans and a lettuce salad with cherry tomatoes. For dessert they had blueberry cream cheese dessert and shoe-fly cupcakes. Chuck had brought his coffeepot and made plenty of fresh-brewed coffee over the campfire he had made.

After lunch we all went for a hike. Kermit sat Henry on his shoulders and Hannah trotted happily along. Chuck had his big walking stick, and seemed to be enjoying himself immensely, for he's a natural-born outdoorsman. Helen and Rosalie had their binoculars and were scanning the treetops for birds and letting Treva take a peek every now and then. We saw a stately buck leaping up over a log and bound away into the thickets, and a little later we saw a few doe and a button buck. We stopped on the banks of the Swift River, watching the white water tumbling and rushing headlong over the rocks. It was a scenic spot, with magnificent pines and the big, blue sky overhead.

Later, back at the campsite, Chuck got started on telling some of his experiences in his boyhood days in the Canadian wilderness, where the bears and panthers were still roaming the woods surrounding their sheep ranch. Maybe sometime I'll take the time to write down some of his exciting stories. Afterward Helen and Rosalie took me up to their house to show me the comforter they have in the frame in their living room and I sat down and helped put in knots for awhile. They are two jolly sisters, utterly devoted to each other and yet they tease and banter playfully.

The others all came up to the Wert house later, for iced tea and delicious crunch bars. Kermit thought they were really good, so I copied the recipe:

Krispy Krunch Bars

Batter:

1/2 cup butter	2 eggs
1 cup brown sugar	1 teaspoon vanilla

1 1/2 cups oatmeal   1 1/4 cups flour
1 teaspoon soda

*Mix all together and spread one-half of it in a 9x13 inch cake pan.
Set the rest aside. Melt one cup chocolate chips in top of double
boiler, and stir in one-half cup peanut butter and two cups rice
krispies and one cup mini-marshmallows. Spread this mixture
over the dough in the pan and drop the remaining dough by tea-
spoonful over top. Bake at 350 degrees for 35 minutes or until done.*

September 17

Sadie was here for a short, but sweet, visit. She's in Minne-
sota with the Bontragers these days and had a way to come with a
vanload. She's still the same wonderful gal. Her arrival is like a
cheerful warmth. She stays awhile and we are content, for she sheds
light on dark days. (I won't write in my journal about the "*hemveh*"
I've had already since I'm here, but, luckily, it was short-lived.)
Sadie brightened the two days she was here (immeasurably) and
even helped with the fall housecleaning. When there's work to be
done, she rolls up her sleeves and pitches right in. (More golden
moments to help fill up our precious memories chest.)

Kermit and Chuck are very busy these days rounding up and
moving the cattle into their winter pastures. Kermit loves being a
cowboy, and I like it better too, seeing him on horseback doing
what he likes to do, if only there weren't those big, crafty range
bulls. I'll be glad when the work is finished, and the bulls wander
off into the hills where they belong.

Verses for Today:
*Our years are like the shadows,
On sunny hills that lie,
Or grasses in the meadows,
That blossom but to die.*

*Lord, crown our faith's endeavor,
With beauty and with grace,
Till, clothed in light forever,
We see Thee face to face.*

It looks like we'll have an early winter, according to the old-timers around here. Oh well, I think we're ready, for Kermit says the fall work is caught after. My housecleaning is done, the fallen leaves are all raked, and the pumpkins are all gathered. Hard frosts are the usual thing, and ofttimes the feel of snow is in the gray skies. The Mullets brought us all the cider we wanted, and boxes and boxes of grapes to be made into juice. The bin in the cellar is filled with apples, and we'll have many a cozy evening by the fire, with apples and popcorn to munch on.

Kermit is well-pleased with the growing season we had and Pop Mullet says the cattle are in fine shape. There's so much to be thankful for! Hannah and Henry are healthy and growing and there's never a dull moment between them (except when they're asleep). Henry's been walking by himself ever since his first birthday and together, they're keeping things lively.

WHAT MORE?

Could any mother wish for more?
I stand beside my open door,
And look out on a world so grand.
And yet confused on ev'ry hand;
I wonder what the future holds,
For you, my child, as the scene unfolds,
And in my heart there is just one prayer,
"May God go with you everywhere."

There are many things I could wish for you;
And some of them might even come true.
But I won't build castles that crumble and fall,
For that would never do at all.
Dreams are made of such gossamer stuff,
That they vanish at even the slightest puff.
And so, in my heart there's just one prayer,
"May God go with you everywhere."

Snow! Heaps of it. Kermit and I made the long trip to Little Falls for our winter's supply of groceries and on the way home, the blizzard began! It was lovely, but we were thankful to be nearly home. I'm so glad we have our provisions, for we might be snowed in for awhile.

On Thanksgiving Day we were invited to the Mullets for a turkey dinner with all the fixings, a real feast! Treva stays there for the winter, but she will come back in March, in time for the calving season. It will be nice to be by ourselves over the winter, but we'll be glad for her help again in the spring.

At Little Falls they had already put up a big Christmas tree in the town square, and Christmas carols were being sung everywhere, even in the stores. I'm glad I have all the Christmas gifts ready and wrapped.

> *Joy to the world, the Lord is come,*
> *Let earth receive her King.*
> *Let every heart, prepare Him room,*
> *And Heaven and nature sing.*

December 1

We visited the Wert sisters last night. We bundled up in layers and went the long way 'round on the sleigh. The myriads of stars were twinkling in the dusky sky and a big full moon came up over the horizon. A lone coyote was howling to the moon from a pine-covered ridge.

I suggested that we sing Christmas carols, the beloved joyous tunes of the season. And so we did, till the frosty air rang with melody. We sang, "It Came Upon the Midnight Clear," "Silent Night," "O Come All Ye Faithful, and "Beautiful Star of Bethlehem." We were snug and warm under the carriage robes, but Hannah kept insisting on peeking out at the lovely, starry night, and I can't blame her.

We surprised the sisters—we caught them out on the lawn having a snowball battle, and they had even made a snowman.

"We're children at heart," Helen explained, a bit embarrassed, but laughing merrily.

"We're in good spirits tonight, for we just received a Christmas gift from our parents—plane tickets to come home for Christmas! Home to Berks County, Pennsylvania, and the rest of the family!"

Rosalie served us spiced cider and cinnamon rolls, and we all sat around the table as the sisters reminisced about their childhood home. Our backgrounds are very similar. They grew up on homegrown garden veggies, *schmeircase* (cup cheese), chow chow, *ponhaus*, sauerkraut, apple butter cooked in a copper kettle, shoefly pie, and even *schnitz boi* (dried apple pie) too. For years they went with their parents to market every week. They had a stand there and sold garden produce; watercress from the spring in their meadow, bacon and hams cured in their smokehouse, dried corn, apples, peaches, pears, dried *schnitz*, shoe-fly, and *schnitz boi*.

Their ancestors were also staunch, God-fearing, honest, and thrifty people who tilled the land and helped it to bring forth its best. The Wert's big farmhouse was also of native stone, and the barn was a Swiss-style, built to last several centuries. Their parents still have the old-fashioned Dutch dialect, but no longer dress plain, and they use modern conveniences like cars and electricity. Helen and Rosalie say they understand Dutch, but can't speak it. Maybe they're afraid we'd have to smile at their mistakes. All this reminiscing almost made me homesick for good ol' PA, but I like it here in Montana and wouldn't wish to move back.

The sisters took us upstairs and showed us a few of their antiques handed down from their grandparents. There was a quaint dower-chest painted with tulips, hearts, and doves; a colorful fractur painting; a *Tauf-scheine*; a *Geburts-scheine*; a chest of drawers painted with pomegranates; and old-fashioned painted plates—all an antique-lover's dream!

They also, at one time, had a *Himmels-brief* (a letter which was supposed to have come directly from above). Someone had given it to them anonymously, with a letter of warning enclosed. If you kept the *Himmels-brief* in your house, you would be protected from lightening, fire, and storms. If you destroyed it, you would be in danger of great harm befalling you and evil would plague you. Old Mr. Wert didn't believe in it so he tossed it right into the fire. Rosalie confessed that for a few weeks afterward she had a great fear that their house would catch fire, and was afraid to go to sleep at night. But nothing of the sort happened, and after awhile she forgot about it.

I asked the sisters what made them choose to move out here, when their childhood roots were in Pennsylvania. Their answer— they were in search of adventure. Helen jokingly said, "Who knows, perhaps in a few years we'll move to Texas, or California, or even Europe." Well, I hope not. It's good to have jolly, friendly neighbors like them.

The ride home was another thrill, all too short, and then bedtime for the little ones. Kermit and I sat by the fire until late, reminiscing about our own childhoods, and we got to talking about Great-Grandmother Feronica and her daughter (one less great-grandmother) Julia and their journals. In Grandma Gertrude's last letter, it sounded like she had a surprise for me coming soon. I do hope it's another journal! Well, we'll just have to wait and see!

Golden Gem for today:
> *Let this thought comfort you: Amid failure, discord, strife, suffering, even now may friends and angels be prepared to sound the chorus, "It is finished." Do not feel, when adverse things happen, that you have failed, or are not being guided, but remember that Jesus said, "In the world ye shall have tribulation, but be of good courage, I have overcome the world."*

December 5

I got that expected package from Grandma Gertrude in the mail today, and I eagerly tore off the wrappings, wondering if it really was another journal. It felt like one and yes, it was! A copybook containing an old journal! How very excited I was to discover that it was another of Julia Glauner's journals. She is the one who wrote the *Majestic Oaks Memoirs*! I wonder how she was able to get another copybook, for I know that in those days (early 1800s) paper wasn't easy to get. Grandma Gertrude sent a letter

with the journal, explaining that Julia and George and their three
children had later moved to Kentucky. Years later their grand-
daughter found the old journal back in a corner on the rafters in
the loft, when the old cabin home was dismantled . It was the first
home that George had built for his family in Kentucky. A relative
sent it to Grandma Gertrude and she had her housekeeper
decipher and recopy the faded handwriting. She wants her copy
of it back, so I'll copy it into my journal for a keepsake for the
family. I'm glad that it's wintertime, and even that we are having
another blizzard, for it gives me time to work on copying the
journal. But first I want to read it, and find out what the wilds of
Kentucky were like. I'm sure there were many dangers and hardships.

December 12

Kermit and I read through Julia's journal together, reading a portion of it each evening after the children were in bed. Now
I'm ready to copy it into my journal. It's a story of trials and heartaches intermingled with joys and sunshine. I think for awhile there
she thought that the sun would never shine again, after her great
sorrow and when the storm clouds became ever darker, but eventually her days became brighter and the load lighter. I had to wonder what her life would have been like, had Abe Rittenhouse chosen her for his wife instead of Margaret Bucher. Julia had her heart
set on him while she was living there in the Conestoga Valley. She
thought her disappointment was too great to bear, but all things
work together for good when one follows the Lord's leading. When
she gave up her own will, peace and happiness followed. And now
I'll copy Julia's journal as I get time, during the coming winter
months when the snow flies and piles in deep drifts on our
Montana homestead. Winters are long here in the Swift River area,
with the lawns and gardens dormant until spring, and the house cozy
and warm. I'll copy Julia's journal in its entirety with no more entries
of my own, except maybe a few at the end if there is room, for I'm
sure that her story is more interesting.

Julia doesn't always have the date with her entries, perhaps
they lost track of what day it was there in the Kentucky wilderness, surrounded by dense woods, without any near neighbors and

with only the prowling bears, squalling wildcats, and graceful deer for company. She could not even write letters to her family back home in Pennsylvania, nor receive any from them, for there was no mail service in those days. How brave those early pioneers must have been, and how much lonesomeness they must have endured at times. It went a long time until they even had as much as a lamp to light their cabin at night! Before that it was just candles. There! I've thought of a name for her story—"Lamplight on the Hearth." I'll add one more Golden Gem, and then all of Julia's journal will follow.

Golden gem:
> *Heavenly Father, help us through poverty to plenty, through unrest to rest, through sorrow to joy, through failure to victory, and through weakness to power.*

JULIA'S JOURNAL BEGINS

What a time to begin a new journal—in the middle of a June thunderstorm. Lightening is flashing, thunder is crashing, the wind is moaning around the corners of the cabin, the rain is beating down on the roof, and my heart quivers with pain, remembering that other thunderstorm that changed our lives forever. I'm thankful that Josiah, Abigail, and baby Aimee are snug in their beds, fast asleep and undisturbed by the storm.

My thoughts wander to the lonely grave on the hill, just east of the cabin, newly made just 6 weeks ago, and the tears course down over my cheeks. George, my beloved, if only he would be here yet, and I wouldn't need to be alone here in these big woods with my three little children. Life is so hard, so tiresome, and if it weren't for the babes, I'm afraid I wouldn't have the courage to go on. We hadn't been here in Kentucky yet a year when that stroke of lightening hit the barn on that fateful night, and set it afire. We didn't see it right away, till the flames were high. George rushed to get the horses out of the burning barn. It was when he was leading out the first horse, my Chief, that we had bought from my uncle, that the burning timber crashed down on them. I could do nothing but weep and wail in that awful time before the neighbors arrived. Jotham and Opal Alden, our nearest neighbors (three miles away) came first, then the four other neighbors that live within five miles of us. The women wept with me, and then in the days that followed the men did all they could have done. They cleared away the debris and built another barn, then plowed the fields and planted the corn, and presented me with another cow and two shoats. But then they left, and the loneliness was nigh unbearable at times, and still is.

Today a peddler man came along, and I anxiously counted what little money I had, then went out to his wagon and selected the barest of necessities—needles and thread, and some calico for clothes. The peddler man was a kindly old soul, he had come straight here from the Aldens and learned of my sad plight. I looked admiringly at the shiny pots and pans, tinware, and other luxuries, and then I spied this copybook. I longingly paged through it, knowing I'd never be able to afford it. What a surprise I had, when I was ready to pay my purchases, the peddler waved my money aside and told me I owe him nothing! It brought tears to my eyes, and blurting out my thanks, I stumbled blindly into the house. It wasn't until I was at the door that I noticed the copybook beneath the cloth. Thinking it was put there by mistake, I rushed back to the wagon with it and handed it back. But the twinkly-eyed old man just smiled and gave it right back, telling me to keep it as his gift to me.

People have been so kind, and we are not forsaken. Sometimes a whole week goes by that I haven't another adult to talk to, but I can take it to the Lord in prayer, and now I can pour out my feelings in my journal, too. I have my Bible and my hymnbook, and even though there's no church house in this area yet, we gather for services on Sundays to sing and pray and worship together. Jotham and Opal Alden kindly come and pick up me and the children in their big wagon with their two horses hitched and ofttimes we stay with them for supper, too. What a blessing that is to my grief-wracked soul, and I hardly know how I'd survive without them.

Ya well, my candle is sputtering, and I see that the thunder-storm is moving around to the south. The rain has slackened to a slow drizzle and the rumblings of thunder are fading away, so it's time to get some sleep before baby Aimee awakens for her night feeding. She's four months old, and her coos and smiles do much to cheer me. Five-year-old Josiah and four-year-old Abigail are a blessing to me, too. They all gladden my heart and give me something to live for. Someday, Lord willing, Josiah will be able to take over the plowing and planting and the clearing of more land, and then things will go better. I must remind myself continually to count my blessings and to thank God daily for children. I'll copy a hymn yet, then head for my lonely bed.

Hymn for today:

God sends His showers of blessing down,
To cheer the plains below;
He makes the grass the mountain's crown,
And corn in valleys grow.

The changing wind, the flying cloud,
Obey His mighty word;
With songs and honors sounding loud,
Praise ye the sovereign Lord.

Late June—I've put the babies to bed, and now I'm sitting out here on the stone doorstep, watching the dusky twilight descending. Soon now it will be too dark to see to be able to write. The fireflies are flickering in and out among the trees, night insects are chorusing, and from down in the swamp comes the croaking of bullfrogs. All is so peaceful; peaceful and lonely.

Warding off the blues has been kind of a losing battle today. I've been trying to think only of the good things, such as the neighbor men coming to hoe the corn, and their women coming along to help me with my work and to cheer me up. Jotham and Opal faithfully come every week to see if I need anything. But try as I might, I can't keep from letting doubts and worries creep into my mind. What will we do when winter comes? What if a howling blizzard comes, and I have to go out to the barn to feed the livestock and leave the little ones inside

alone? What if something should happen to me, and my little ones would starve?

There have been blizzards here I know, although it doesn't happen often. What if I'd lose my way and get lost in the woods, perishing in the storm, with no one to care for my babes? And oh, what if one of them should get sick and I'd have to go for help, leaving them all alone, frightened and worried? What if a bear should break into the stable and kill the cow and shoats?

I know it's wrong to worry, I must put my trust in God that He will take care of us and provide for our needs. Maybe it's just when I'm overtired that these discouraging thoughts plague me so. I'm tired in every bone, from hoeing corn hour after hour tonight, while Abigail entertained Aimee in her basket under the tree. My thoughts just wanted to dwell on the story Aunt Tilda told me years ago about one of our long-ago grandmothers leaving her baby in a basket out beside the cabin as she worked in the garden. Their faithful dog kept guard, but alas, a band of warriors sent an arrow through the dog and stole the baby. I shudder as I think of it, for there are still some Indians in these parts. That's another one of my fears; that sometime I'll come back into our cabin and find my little ones gone—stolen by Indians, or wandered away and gotten lost in the woods—even torn by a bear or wolves, like my step-brother Tommy was years ago. Oh, how I long to have the comfort of George's presence. How he used to laugh at my fears and make me feel at ease.

Last night I dreamt that George had come back. It was so real with his twinkling hazel eyes and charming smile. What a blow to wake up to the realization that it will never happen. I suppose my lot in life will always be tears, sighs, and longings, and fears, and worries. Oh, for a deeper faith—one that never doubts, never fears, only a deep, abiding trust that all will be well. Perhaps copying a verse out of Psalms will comfort me.

"For Thou wilt light my candle: The Lord my God will lighten my darkness. For by Thee I have run through a troop; and by my God have I leaped over a wall. As for God, His way is perfect: The Word of the Lord is tried: He is a buckler to all those that trust in Him."

July—The field corn is growing so sturdy, green, and tall. How George's heart would have rejoiced to see it. He loved this land with its clear, rippling streams, misty ridges, blue skies, and the abundant wildlife. The pheasants, wild turkeys, deer, and rabbits are plentiful in the thickets, and to him, going hunting was a pleasure. He dreamed of clearing more land every year and of the crops growing luxuriantly in the dark, rich earth. But now, who will chop down these great trees on our land? Jotham Alden and the other neighbors have all they can do to clear their own fields.

I feel so bereft sometimes, but I do want to trust in God, that He will provide for us. So I'll rejoice in the beauties of each season—the valleys of bluets and buttercups, the violets and daisies, woodlands of bouncing bets, dogwoods and laurel. In the spring there are brilliant patches of rhododendrons and azaleas. Flowers are food for the soul, or at least, they inspire you to beautiful thoughts and inspirations.

George called this a land of milk and honey, and he intended to do his best to bring out the good in it. But what can a poor struggling widow do, with three little children to care for? Now, now! Enough of morbid broodings, for I do want to go on in faith and courage, to bear up under the load for the children's sake. Josiah helped nicely with the hoeing, keeping at it longer than I dared hope, until he tired. He's a miniature George, both in looks and in pluck. And Abigail did very well, too, in entertaining Baby by singing to her and rocking the cradle, which I had set out close to the field.

It's growing dark now, and a cool, refreshing breeze has sprung up. A song sparrow's singing its evening vespers, and the whippoorwills are calling from shadowy rills. I'll take the time to copy a hymn yet, if there's still enough light to see by. How I wish I'd have a lamp to set on the mantle above the hearth, to bring cheer and light to our cabin home. Candles sputter and flicker so dreadfully that it makes a room seem spooky and frightening when I'm feeling low. But there! I didn't mean to complain, for I'm really very thankful for candles. Now for the hymn:

> *The Lord my Shepherd is,*
> *I shall be well-supplied,*
> *Since He is mine and I am His,*
> *What can I want beside?*
>
> *He leads me to the place,*
> *Where heavenly pasture grows,*
> *Where living waters gently pass,*
> *And full salvation flows.*

August—A beautiful Sunday. Jotham and Opal Alden came for us this morning with two fine horses hitched to the wagon and took us along to services at the Kitzmiller homestead. How I loved the ride, sitting with my three children on the back of the wagon among the five Alden youngsters. There's ten-year-old Jeff, nine-year-old Mitsy, six-year-old Ephie, four-year-old Joth, and baby Opal. They're well-behaved children and have been taught nice manners.

The weather was surprisingly cool again after our prolonged, wearisome heat wave. An all-day rain yesterday refreshed the thirsty earth, and this morning's sunshine dazzled on the sparkling grass and leaves. The sky was a lovely clear blue, and everything smelled so fresh and alive again as we followed the path through the woods. The horses were stepping lively, upheaded and eager, and I just feasted my eyes on them.

How I have missed our horses since . . . since the fire. The horse stalls in the new barn are still empty, and there's a sad desolate feeling there, with no whinnies, no stamping in the stall, and no friendly nuzzling and nickering for oats. Also horses make me think of George, and then the tears insist on coming. Sigh.

Jotham and Opal sang hymns as we drove, and my heart rejoiced to hear the comforting words. They sang, "I'll Praise My Maker," "How Endless Is Thy Love," "Joyful We Thank and Praise Thee," and "Bless the Lord, O My Soul." The children sang along too, and how their clear, childish voices rang out and reverberated through the woods. I imagined what it would be like to hear the peals of church bells ringing, inviting all the neighborhood to come and worship. Will we ever have a church here in the midst of the wilderness?

The Kitzmiller homestead is one of the oldest in the valley, or rather, here the longest. They have ten children so they've already added several more rooms to their cabin, cleared acres and acres of land, and built a big new barn. All this had been the hopes and dreams of George, too. I had to brush away a few tears thinking about it, when we drove in at their homestead. How soon our dreams can come to naught and dashed to pieces and only the broken fragments remain to be gathered.

Five other families gathered there in the Kitzmiller's big front room. A new family just arrived last week and for two hours we all sat on the backless plank benches to worship. First we sang hymns; then Josiah read several chapters out of the Bible, in his deep, reverent voice; and afterward we knelt to pray together. Our services are not what they'd be if we had a preacher, but they still give us a fresh courage to go on in our spiritual lives, and to not grow faint and weary.

At noon the men stretched out the table to its full length there under the trees, and we women put on the big tablecloth and spread our eats on it—loaves of crusty bread, hickory-smoked hams, a crock of cup cheese, pickled beets and eggs, honey and apple butter, plum preserves, pudding, and molasses cakes. To me it was a real feast, and the fellowshipping with the other women made it taste all the better.

They're a real kind and friendly bunch, especially Opal. She's so thoughtful and always generous and unselfish. She has gone through heartaches also, for they have a graveyard on the hillside near their cabin, too. Their oldest son lived to be just two years old, and died of a fever. Their next child was a girl who was never healthy and died at the age of 16 months. I hugged my little Aimee to myself just thinking about it, and thanked God for her good health.

After the dishes were washed, we women sat out under the shade tree to visit, sharing our daily lives and tidbits of what scarce news we can get from the surrounding territory. Mrs. Kitzmiller said that just last week one of the settlers in these parts, living ten miles from here, Shem Decimas by name, lost his wife. She happened to chop herself in the leg with a scythe, and infection and gangrene set in. He has six motherless children now, and he's not the church-going kind. Poor man, I feel for him so, and without a faith to help sustain him. Those poor, poor children. May we remember the family in our prayers daily. Time for a Bible verse:

"In Thee, O Lord, do I put my trust; Let me never be put to confusion. Deliver me in Thy righteousness and cause me to escape; incline Thine ear unto me, and save me. Be thou my strong habitation whereunto I may continually resort; Thou has given commandment to save me; for Thou art my rock and my fortress." (Psalm 71:1-3)

September—Harvest time is here, and a large orange harvest moon is rising up over the treetops as I sit here on the stone doorstep enjoying the peace and coolness of the evening. My candle flickers in the breeze, but I am thankful for the light it sheds. Josiah sat with me for awhile chattering away, asking questions, and marveling at the shadows and sounds of the night. But soon his nodding head drooped against my shoulder and I sent him to his bed, where the girls were already in dreamland.

Today the neighbors gathered here to bring in the harvest and how my heart soars with praise and thankfulness! The barn and the granary are filled, with plenty for the shoats and cow, and the seed corn has been saved for planting. Perhaps soon I'll be able to somehow get some horses again, and then I can plow my own fields and plant corn, beans, squash, and turnips.

Tonight as I milked the cow, she mooed plaintively, and swished her tail in my face, as if to say, "I'll take some of that pile of pumpkins, please, for my supper." I could have said, "Not yet, Bossy, we'll have to see if there's any left to spare for you." In the loft I've strung up lots of strings of onions which help to make the wild game taste so much better. I'm also storing bags and bags of dried beans and corn in the loft and in the root cellar there are heaps of beets, carrots, cabbages, and turnips.

While the menfolk helped bring in the harvest, the womenfolk knotted a comforter for the Shem Decimas family, the ones who lost their mother. Opal Alden had pieced it together with scraps of brightly dyed sacking. It was a good feeling to be able to do something for those motherless children. Shem had come for awhile in the afternoon to help with the harvest, too, and before he left, Jotham brought him into the house. With a stammering of thanks he gratefully accepted the gift of the comforter, then came to shake hands with me. He has a brown, craggy face, and as he peered at me from under his bushy brows, he said, "I wish you well. I wish you an awful lot of good luck." Then he turned abruptly, got on his horse and rode away. It seemed like a strange thing to say. What good would wishing someone luck do? Perhaps he said it to show how he felt. Jotham was the last to leave and when he came to the doorway to tell Opal he was ready to go, he spoke a few encouraging words to me, too. How it cheers me that the neighbors were willing to do this for me. I feel light-hearted tonight, like singing a hymn of praise. Instead I'll copy one in my journal:

> *Jesus shall reign where'er the sun,*
> *Doth His successive journeys run;*
> *His kingdoms stretch from shore to shore,*
> *Till moons shall wax and wane no more.*
> *For Him shall endless prayers be made,*
> *And praises throng to crown His head;*
> *His name, like sweet perfume shall rise,*
> *With every morning sacrifice.*

October—Wild geese are winging their way southward, and frost has nipped the last of the weeds in the garden. Soon the chilly winds of winter will blow, but right now we're still having clear, blue-sky weather.

I had a visitor tonight who came on horseback after the children were in bed. My heart gave a lurch when I saw that it was Shem Decimas, for I could guess what he might want. I was right, and so soon after his wife died! Why, it's scarcely two months she's in her grave and I told him it's much too soon for him to be knowing his mind about asking another woman for her hand in marriage. And George has only been gone for a half year. He said he knows it all too well that it's too soon, but his children are running wild and the work is piling up. Their clothes are in tatters and their meals are poorly prepared. I felt sorry for him, but I had to send him away. What else could I have done?

After he left, I got my shawl and sat on the doorstep for a long time, staring mournfully out into the shadows. I know I could never love another man again, but perhaps I could at least be a mother to those poor motherless waifs and cook the meals. According to what I've heard, he's one of the more well-to-do settlers, he has plenty of land and a large comfortable house. The coming winter dreads me so—just the thought of it plain down discourages me. I know I must trust the Lord to take care of us, but how can I know whether this isn't in His plans for me? I'll have to pray and seek His will.

Shem is a tall, heavy-set man with coarse features, but he has a polite way of talking. Perhaps he would make a good father for Josiah, Abigail, and Aimee. I sat there dreaming for a long time. I would see to it that he would come to church services and become a true believer, and we would lead the children in the right paths. In glowing dreams I imagined myself as a heroine, doing much good for the family, and as mistress of the Decimas home, looking well to the ways of the household, and in my tongue being the law of kindness, as it says in Proverbs 31. But then, with a sigh, I remembered that the lot of a stepmother is not the easiest and the cares would be many and heavy to bear. Oh well, perhaps he will soon find someone else to ask. Time for a Bible verse:

"Her candle goeth not out by night, she layeth her hands to the spindle and her hands hold the distaff. She stretcheth out her hand to the poor; yea, she

reacheth forth with her hand to the needy. Strength and honor are her clothing and she shall rejoice in time to come."(Proverbs 31:18-20, 25)

November—My heart is heavy as I write this, for fears and doubts assail me and I find it nigh impossible to trust. The wind is raw and moaning, rattling around the chimney and the corners of the cabin tonight, scattering dried leaves as it goes. Last night we had another calamity. I had tucked the children into their beds early, and weary from laundry and soap-making day, climbed into the straw tick early myself. I had already drifted off to a peaceful slumber, when deafening crashes and agonizing screams jerked me back to reality. It was the pigs screaming in pain and terror! I grabbed the gun and fearfully headed for the stable. The door was splintered and by the light of the moon I saw a huge bear emerge and run off into the shadows, carrying a shoat under each "arm." I fired a shot after it, but must have missed for he disappeared into the night, and that was the last I saw of the bear and the pigs. At least the frightened cow was safe, and the children had slept through it all. I barricaded the stable doorway with logs, as best as I could, all the while casting fearful glances behind me. I supposed the bear was sated by then, with all the pork it could eat in one night. The rest of the night was a long, sleepless vigil, though, full of tears and dread.

This forenoon after I had put Aimee down for her morning nap, I gave Josiah and Abigail the button jar to play with, and gave them strict orders to play quietly **inside** the cabin until I returned. I took the gun and hurried the three miles to the Aldens as fast as I could, frightening the pheasants and bunnies that were out for their morning strolls and hops. My lungs felt nigh to bursting when I arrived, and it was all I could do to gasp out my story, but Jotham kindly dropped everything and came to my rescue. He quickly loaded some split and hewn logs and the axe onto his wagon and hitched his horses, while Opal prepared her family to come along. Thoughtful as always, she took the pot of beans and ham she had simmering on the hearth, and brought them along, too, for our dinner. They knew I was anxious about my little ones and wasted no time in returning with me. Oh, how can I ever repay them for all they do for me? They'll have their reward in Heaven someday. Jostling around on the back of the wagon, I made up my mind

that if Shem Decimas comes back and asks again for
my hand in marriage, I will say yes. It's not nice to be so
dependent on others for help, and so beholden to them.
To have a man to provide for me and the babes again
would be wonderful, for such a burden was not meant
for a woman alone.

Jotham fixed the stable door twice as sturdy as it was before while Opal and I worked at knitting stockings. We had her beans and ham for dinner, along with some of my fresh bread and apple butter and apple pudding and milk. At the table I told them about Shem's offer of marriage, and that I had decided to accept. I saw Jotham and Opal exchange troubled glances, and then Jotham, without a word, arose and got down my Bible from the shelf and opened it to 2 Corinthians 6 and in his deep, rich voice read verses 14 and 15:

> *"Be not unequally yoked together with unbelievers, for what fellowship hath righteousness with unrighteousness? And what communion hath light with darkness? And what part hath he that believeth with an infidel?"*

He kindly explained that Shem is an unbeliever, even an infidel, and that some of his dealings with the other settlers haven't been the nicest, rather on the shady side. He advised me to tell him that because of that I can't accept his offer. He said that he and Opal would do all they can for me, and see that I and the children would be provided for. That gave me something to ponder over, for I certainly don't want to disobey one of Christ's commands. I feel utterly discouraged tonight, for with the winter coming, how will we cope? And now we'll have no hogs to butcher, no hams, bacon, *ponhaus*, or pork. Maybe copying a hymn will encourage and cheer me.

> *Religion bears our spirits up,*
> *While we expect that blessed hope;*
> *The bright appearance of the Lord,*
> *And faith stands leaning on His word.*

December—Trouble, trouble everywhere. Now there are talks about an impending Indian attack again, after a year of fairly quiet and peaceful times. Also, the children have been sick and croupy, barking almost like little dogs.

This has been a long and dreary week, and I find that hope and trust have dried up and flown away, like the dried leaves in the wind. It seems like I can't even find comfort in prayer anymore. Ever since Jotham told me it would be wrong to marry Shem Decimas, I have been in a quandary . One moment I decide that he is right, and the next moment I'm sure that God's blessings would be in it, for then I could lead those six motherless children to faith and the right, and perhaps even be able to help Shem to see the light and become a churchgoer. Would that not be a noble mission?

Then tonight little Aimee had a choking spell, and there for a time I was sure I would lose her, for her croup was so bad. In a panic, I made a steam tent with a blanket around a pot of boiling water. She gasped and choked, then turned blue—oh, so very blue. Finally, she was able to cough up what was choking her. The crisis was over and she fell into a peaceful sleep. I laid her in the cradle, then crept to the rug in front of the hearth and with my head down on my arms, burst into tears. I cried as I hadn't cried since the early weeks after George's death.

In the midst of my storm of tears, there came a knock on the door. In dismay, I blotted my tears away and went to answer it. There on the doorstep stood Shem, hat in hand, asking if he could come in. Seeing my tears, he hastened to comfort me, saying that all he owned would be mine and that I would never want for anything again if I'd accept his offer. He would provide for us in everything, and I'd have nothing to fear. His offer was so tempting that I burst into tears again, but after I got a hold of myself, I told him that I could never marry an unbeliever. He looked shocked and said that he is NOT an unbeliever, and that he wants to start coming to church as soon as we are married. He said he would take us all to services every Sunday, if I so wish.

After much persuasive talking, and scaring me more about the danger of an Indian attack when I'm here alone in the woods with my babes, I finally said I would marry him at the proper time, since it's only four months after his wife died and it's still too soon. But he insisted that it would be better for the children if we marry now, and that he would go for a preacher right away—which could take quite awhile. Seeing that I had no further arguments, he left right away, perhaps fearing I'd change my mind again. I had another crying spell after he left, and I still have no peace and happiness about it, perhaps because I've disregarded Jotham's kind advice. But, oh, he doesn't know what it's like being so very alone and needy. How does he know that in this case it may not be what God wants me to do, and that I could do that family a tremendous lot of good?

"O Lord God of my salvation, I have cried day and night before Thee: incline Thine ear unto my cry, for my soul is full of troubles and my life draweth nigh unto the grave." (Psalm 66:1-3)

Part Three

Journey Through Tears

January—For richer or poorer, for better or worse, I am now Mrs. Shem Decimas. What's done is done and cannot be undone, therefore there will be no more wavering, but come what may, I will make the best of things. It was perhaps three weeks after my last journal entry that Shem arrived on my doorstep one evening with a circuit rider preacher, and almost before I knew what had happened the ceremony was performed and the knot tied. The preacher had come on horseback, and left as soon as he had gotten his pay, for he was needed in Rock Springs, 20 miles away. He, I rather thought, didn't seem much like a preacher, but he assured me that indeed he is a parson.

Shem had come on his two-horse wagon and stayed the night. The next day we loaded all my belongings and I and the children moved to the Decimas home. At once I got busy cleaning the house, and cooking and baking. There are five boys and one girl in this family. Callie's the youngest, a pretty little thing, 3 years of age. The two oldest boys, Rufe and Lars, ages 13 and 12, have been doing the cooking and I'm sure they're very glad to hand over the responsibility. Next are Jess, 10, Nat, 7, and Jan, 5. The boys, unlike their Papa, look a bit thin and peaked, and are all very shy. Josiah and Jan are the same age and already good friends. Callie and Abigail are a year apart in age, and do play together some, but have done some scrapping, too.

In the week since I've been here, I cleaned the house from top to bottom and now it's finally beginning to seem like home. There are four big rooms downstairs, plus a wash house, and two rooms upstairs. And wonder of wonders, there's a real iron cookstove in the kitchen. I never thought I'd ever get to use one of those.

The youngsters all need new clothes, so that will keep me really busy over the winter months, along with my other household duties. Shem is usually away all day. He leaves early in the morning and comes home for supper, but often late even for that, and must reheat what

I saved for him. He's a man of few words, but now my worries of providing for the little ones and of the dangers of being alone are over. Come spring, he will also farm George's fields, which will make him rather busy, but the boys are growing up and will soon need more work. I'll copy a hymn of rejoicing tonight:

O for a thousand tongues to sing,
My dear Redeemer's praise;
The glories of my God and King,
The triumph of His grace!

My gracious Master and my God,
Assist me to proclaim,
To spread through all the earth abroad,
The honors of Thy name.

January 12—Shem has a calendar hanging on the wall, so I'll be able to put in the dates of my diary entries after this. Yesterday was Sunday, and we didn't get to church after all. Shem didn't get in until late on Saturday night, because he said he had trouble with his cattle stampeding. He slept in the barn so he could keep an eye on them. Then this morning he didn't feel well, and he slept all day, or so it seemed. So the five younger ones and I had some Bible storytelling sessions but the four oldest ones disappeared as soon as the chores were done and breakfast eaten. I saw nothing of them until suppertime.

It was then that I discovered that they had raided the cellar and helped themselves to whatever they wanted. (Sigh) There will have to be some law and order enforced around here and the sooner the better. When I pulled up the dumbwaiter I discovered that two of my squash pies were gone, a loaf of bread I'd baked, and also a jar of pickled red beet eggs I'd prepared. Poor boys, they're thin enough, and I don't begrudge them the vittles, but they should come to the table and do things decently and in order. I have been insisting on bowing our heads for prayer before we eat which was something new for them, and I have to constantly remind them not to reach for things before we say grace.

Shem didn't show up until bedtime and then I was startled to discover that his eyes were bloodshot and he didn't seem well. Oh, dear, let's hope he stays well. This morning he seemed all right again, and went out to work as usual.

There's something about Shem that bothers me. He shows almost no affection to his boys, only little Callie seems to be the apple of his eye. It hurts my heart to see him teasing and tickling her into giggles and yet utterly ignoring his boys and my three. It puts a stab of fear into my heart that they won't really have a father's love and care after all. I'll have to take it to the Lord in prayer. Always, at the back of my mind, is the memory of Jotham's kind, earnest advice and how sure he was of what my decision should be. Did I make a mistake? I'm too tired to think about it now, but I'll take time to copy a Bible verse yet. I'm so thankful I have my Bible, for there was none in this home.

> *"Forever O Lord, Thy word is settled in Heaven. Thy faithfulness is unto all generations: Thou hast established the earth, and it abideth. They continue to this day according to Thine ordinances: For they are Thy servants. Unless Thy law had been my delight, I should then have perished in mine affliction."*
> (Psalm 119:89-92)

January 19—Yesterday was Sunday again, and after pleading with Shem (who was still in bed) to take us all to church and reminding him of his promises, he refused point blank. He turned his face to the wall and in a growly voice called me a nag. He said he was too tired, and that I could hitch the horses and go alone if I considered it so all-fired important.

And so, with tears blinding my eyes and with a heart sunk as low as it could go, I got the little ones ready and with Rufe's help, hitched the horses to the wagon. Lars, Jess, and Nat had disappeared again, even after I had informed them we were all going to church. As soon as the horses were hitched, Rufe was a goner, too.

This was all so different from what I had planned, that all during the six-mile drive the tears flowed unchecked. Shem's horses are thin and unkempt, and appear ill-cared for. They haven't much go-power, so we were the last ones there. At least Jan and Josiah enjoyed the drive and happily jumped off the wagon when we arrived, but Abigail and Callie shyly clung to my skirts.

It took courage to walk in alone, just like I had to when I was a widow, but it was worth it. Opal and the other women welcomed me warmly. How thankful I was that I saw no condemnation in Opal's eyes. I felt like I deserved some chiding and reprimanding. Jotham, too, came to shake hands after the services, and kindly wished me the Lord's blessings. (No condemnation either, even though I had spurned his advice.) It brought tears to my eyes, for I feel as though I'm already reaping and regretting my decision.

The singing greatly cheered and encouraged me. Listening to Jotham reading the scriptures filled me with hope and a feeling of peace, and that God will be with me even though I've made a mistake. We had a good fellowship dinner at noon, and what fun the children had playing together. We womenfolk had such a pleasant visit. I learned that the reported Indian massacre was all a false alarm—there's no danger after all. What a relief!

Right now I feel too tired to write more, even too tired to copy a hymn. Shem has left (I wish I'd know where he goes) and isn't back even though it's past bed-time. I'm tired. Good-night.

February 3—Opal Alden invited me to come to her quilting today. After getting Shem's grudging consent, I got the little ones ready and we went with the two horses and wagon. Rufe and Lars hitch them all by themselves now, and seem glad to do it for me. The way seemed far, and the drive tiresome, but it was a day well-spent, giving me a renewed courage to go on with my lot in life. How refreshing it was to visit with dear Opal and the other wives, and to exchange thoughts and feelings.

On the way home, the boys were delighted when we startled a flock of turkeys out of a thicket by the road-side. They flew up, gobbling in protest. Crossing the creek we saw a buck bounding away into the woods. It was even good to see home again. My heart rejoiced that I am mistress of such a stately house and that the two big barns are ours, too.

My elation was short-lived, however, for Shem was home already and upset that supper wasn't ready. He was in a surly mood and cuffed Rufe on the ear. I cringed as I smelled liquor on his breath and we all scurried around like frightened mice, trying not to aggravate him more. What a relief when he finally sat down to eat and then headed for the barn.

It was after the dishes were washed that the blow came. I went for my Bible to read a portion like I do every evening, but my Bible wasn't there. I questioned the boys, and they, with wide, scared eyes, informed me that a peddler had come round, and Shem had sold my Bible to him for a lot of money. He said that Bibles were all very well for the old and the sick. Oh, what crushing disappointment! Tears and sighing seem to be my portion. It helps me to pour out my woes into my journal and to tell them to the Lord.

I'm thankful I still have my copybook of hymns, which I'll keep hidden from this point on. I'm also thankful that I've memorized a lot of scripture. I'm afraid though I won't always be able to remember which book of the Bible it is from, and which chapter and verse.

For now, I'll copy a hymn:

King of glory! Reign forever,
Thine an everlasting crown;
Nothing from Thy love shall sever,
Thou whom Thou hast made Thine own.

February 17—Shem's big ferocious dog, Trix, seems to have taken a liking to me, maybe because I feed him scraps and treat him kindly. He's used to getting kicked around a lot, and can be very vicious. I tell Josiah and Abigail to keep away from him, for he doesn't take kindly to children, especially not the three newcomers.

It seems to be happening more and more frequent now that Shem comes in somewhat drunk and then we're all afraid of him. Tonight he whipped Lars for spilling the jar of honey and boxed Nat's ears for bumping against the stove grate.

Need I tell you, my journal, how I regret not heeding Jotham's advice? But sighs and tears will not undo it, and I'm here to stay, I fear. I guess I've "made my bed, and now I must lie in it." Gone are my lofty dreams of leading the family in the right paths, for what can a woman do when the head of the house tears everything down she tries to do? Oh, what will become of my little ones now? How can Josiah become a true man when he's overshadowed by Shem's influence? I have sinned by disobeying God in being unequally yoked with an unbeliever, and the way of transgressors is hard.

"Thou hast laid me in the lowest pit, in darkness, in the deeps. Thy wrath lieth hard upon me, and Thou has afflicted me with all Thy waves." (Psalms)

March 21—It's the first day of spring, and it's like a ray of cheer after a long, hard winter, and we are badly in need of some cheer. The frogs chorus down in the marsh, cardinals trill every morning at dawn, and robins sing sweetly all day. I found a patch of wildflowers down by the spring and fresh watercress for supper.

Shem's dog lies here on the porch looking miserable as I sit out here on the step to write. He's had a wound, but seems to be on the way to recovery. It happened one evening last week. After all of us were in bed there came a ruckus outside and shouts for Shem to come out. Trix lay crouched on the porch, and when the riders came close, he leapt for the nearest one, growling viciously and menacingly. A shot was fired, and the injured dog retreated underneath the porch to lick his wound. Shem grabbed his gun and went to the door, and then there were more shouts and threats, arguing and warnings. Finally the riders galloped off, while sending back a volley of shots, probably as a warning. There's a serious feud a-brewing, I'm afraid, and I'm so scared that someone will get killed or badly injured yet.

Shem comes home half drunk more often than not, and the boys disappear one by one. I fear that my son, too, is adversely affected by all this for he seems more insecure and fearful. The day after the armed riders came by, Shem was more surly than ever. When he came in after dark, he told Josiah to bring him his moccasins. He greatly prizes those moccasins (given to him by an Indian) and likes to wear them in the house. Josiah brought them and set them on the bench beside Shem, who was eating his supper by then. Little Aimee, who is walking now, came along and happened to knock them under the table. Josiah went back to his play, and suddenly felt himself flying through the air.

"I SAID, GET ME MY MOCCASINS," Shem yelled as he grabbed Josiah.

"WHY DIDN'T YOU OBEY ME?"

He twisted his ear, demanding an answer. Abigail quickly retrieved the moccasins from under the table, and fearfully thrust them at him. With a knock on the head, Shem dropped the boy and headed for bed. My heart ached for the sobbing Josiah, and for the thousandth time, I wished we'd be back in our cabin home, alone. Would it be wrong for us to go back there? But, oh, I know Shem would just come and take us back and make us suffer all the more for our leaving. O Lord, help us all.

April—April is the month of blooms and blossoms and birdsong, but little do they do to cheer our hearts. Tonight after everyone was in bed except Shem who was still away, I became so burdened that I decided to go for a walk in order to forget my troubles a bit more. A large round moon was shining through the budded trees, and a pair of whippoorwills were calling from afar. A coyote yipped from the hills and an echo came back from across the valley.

I followed the trail through the woods, too burdened to even think of such dangers as rattlesnakes, bears, and bobcats. I was especially burdened because in the past few weeks I've been noticing a lump on my neck, a tumor of some kind. It's not painful, but I can feel it growing and it worries me exceedingly. Oh, if I should die, what would become of my little ones? Who would teach them right from wrong, tell them Bible stories, and take them to church? Would Josiah grow up drinking liquor like Shem, a wicked man? Would he become an unbeliever like Shem? I became so distraught at the thought that I just kept on walking and walking.

Soon I saw a flickering light through the trees and I heard men's voices. I stopped in the shadows and stared. There I saw Shem and four other men sitting around a campfire drinking. Suddenly I knew that they were making liquor on their own and selling it. Sick at heart, I turned away to head for home and accidentally tripped over a tree branch which broke in two. There was a sharp crack and Shem sprang up, gun at the ready.

"Get him, Trix!" he said urgently. "Sic-em!" Trix sprang up, barking ferociously, and I ran blindly. A shot rang out and I heard the whine of the bullet. With a bound the dog was nearly upon me, but suddenly he stopped barking and his tail began to wag. I kept on running for home as fast as I could, while Trix ran along beside me as if protecting me. My breath came in painful gasps and the hurting in my side was agonizing, but I kept on running until I reached the house.

Quietly I let myself in the door and went straight to bed, too spent and weary to even undress. Shem came in a short time later, muttering under his breath about confounded snooping trespassers. He stood his loaded gun by the bed, and probably intended to sleep with one eye open. After he was snoring I gave way to tears. Verily, the way of transgressors is hard. If only I had heeded Jotham's advice.

May 13—I've been driving to church services every Sunday with the younger children because it's the only calm or port I have in a sea of storm. I confided to Opal my fears and worries about this ever-enlarging tumor on my neck and my fear of dying and leaving my poor little lambs in such an environment. She knows it all now. Even about Shem's cruelty and wickedness, and what we must endure. She talked it over with Jotham and they have agreed that they will take my little ones to raise should something happen to me. It's such a relief to me, such a burden off my back. Oh, thank God, the children will be taken care of in a Christian environment.

After church we sat under the shade trees again to do our visiting. I learned that the circuit rider preacher, the one who married us, is back and is holding revival meetings near Rock Springs nearly every evening. Oh, how I'd love to go, but I know that Shem would never allow it on a work day.

Another thing I learned on Sunday was that there's a band of robbers in the area. They steal whatever they can lay their hands on, anything from crocks of honey (at the Kitzmillers), laying hens (at the Aldens), to big things like horses and cattle if it's possible. It makes me shudder, and it would worry me even more were I and the children still alone in our cabin.

I feel so much better tonight, knowing that my three little ones will be taken care of in a Christian home when I die—the world seems like a beautiful place again. The grass is green and lush and dotted with yellow buttercups. The birds are raising their fledglings in their nests and singing sweetly morning and evening, and the flowering bush in the yard is a maze of white blossoming glory. And yet, when I think of Shem's children, my heart aches again. What will become of them? Who will teach them to do right, and be a good example for them? Well, now it's time for a hymn:

> *Come Thou fount of every blessing,*
> *Tune my heart to sing Thy grace.*
> *Streams of mercy never ceasing,*
> *Call for songs of loudest praise.*

June—The wild strawberries are ripe and what delicious jams they make! June is one of the loveliest months, and yet there is no joy and love in our daily life. Shem has been feuding with the neighbors two miles to the north and now they won't speak to each other at all. Oh well, that's better than an angry tirade of shouting.

When the neighbor's cattle strayed over onto our land, Shem shot after them and hit the big bull, killing it on the spot. With his pair of scrawny mules he brought the carcass back here and we had a butchering day. How I loathed it for I knew it wasn't right. But the worst thing that happened was when I said something about it, Shem, in a fit of anger, forbade me to go to church services anymore. Why? He said I was getting too religious for my own good. I cried all the rest of the day, for oh, how I will miss my friend Opal and the other women who attend. Oh, why didn't I heed Jotham's warning? But I never knew Shem was like this. May God forgive me for not seeking more counsel before I blindly plunged into something after being warned. And now I must die for my sins, but even death is a welcome thought.

"Let the sighing of the prisoner come before Thee; according to the greatness of Thy power preserve Thou those that are appointed to die." (Psalm 79)

This tumor on my neck seems to loom like a mountain on my horizon.

August—Two sad and weary months have passed since my last journal entry. Oh, how I've missed being able to go to services and fellowshipping with other believers, especially Opal.

My despised growth keeps growing larger and larger, and how I shrink back from suffering on my deathbed. I've been keeping it covered with a scarf so that Shem won't see it, for he gets angry at any sickness or weakness. I haven't told him how poorly I've been feeling lately, either.

But then on Saturday night, after everyone had taken their weekly bath in the big washtub and was in bed sleeping, I refilled it once more, for now it was my turn to take a refreshing soak in it. Shem came home before I was out of the tub and lit a candle. He took one look at me and said, "Mercy, woman, what's that thing on your neck?" So I told him the truth and that I'd probably die soon. His face blanched, but he made no reply.

On Monday morning he hitched the horses to the wagon, and told me to get ready, for he was taking me to a doctor. A doctor? I hadn't known there was a doctor in these parts, perhaps he had only recently come. Hope stirred anew in my breast, maybe there was a remedy. Wonderingly I got my bonnet and climbed upon the wagon seat beside him.

After we'd gone a few miles I asked him where the doctor lived and what his name was, but there was no reply. The sun beat down mercilessly as it climbed higher and higher into the sky, and the leaves stirred in the hot breeze. We're in the midst of a drought, and the ride wasn't interesting and refreshing like it would've been in the spring. We met a few teamsters on the road, and Shem would nod to them, but when we met the neighbor he was feuding with, he spat disgustedly into the dust and turned his head away without acknowledging him.

The sun was high overhead when the barking of dogs announced that we were getting close to the town of Rock Springs. I looked about curiously for I'd never been to this town before. There was a livery stable, a blacksmith shop, a general store and mercantile, a tavern, a jail, numerous log houses, and the Warden Inn.

Shem put his team in the livery, then curtly told me to follow him. At the far end of town, we stopped at an unkempt-looking place with a shabby rail fence around it. A vicious-looking dog arose from where he was lying in the shade of a catalpa tree and began to growl menacingly. A window opened and a man's surly voice silenced the dog and bade us come in.

The interior of the room we entered was dimly lit and I felt myself shrink back in fear. Was this man really a doctor? Somehow, the situation seemed sinister and frightening, and I wanted to run away. But already Shem was pointing out my ugly growth to the beak-nosed man, the doctor, who had come from the other room and was eyeing us coldly. He had a long, curled moustache and several of his front teeth were missing, making big gaps in his mouth.

He scrutinized me closely for a few nerve-wracking minutes, then said, "Ah, very bad, very bad." He ordered me to lie down on the table in his oily voice. "We must make haste to get rid of this tumor before it strangles you," he said. I suddenly shuddered and shrank back in alarm. Was he going to pull out a big knife and cut the tumor away now? But Shem told me sharply to do what the doctor said and I fearfully climbed onto the table. He pressed his hand first on one side of the growth, then on the other. Then he closed his eyes, and moving his head from one side to the other, began to chant some words, apparently in another language.

Quickly I pushed his hands away and sat up. "Stop!" I cried in alarm. "Maybe you don't know what you're saying." The man looked quite astonished, so I went on, telling him the story that Mother Kettie had once told me.

There was once a blacksmith who had a reputation for being able to tame and control any unruly or unmanageable horse. People who had horses who wouldn't stand still to be shod brought them to him. Before he would begin, he would close his eyes and say some words in another language and then the horse would stand perfectly still until it was shod. One day a Dutchman took his untamable horse to the blacksmith to be shod, and again, before he began, the blacksmith said his unknown words. The Dutchman stopped him abruptly, looking very frightened. He asked the blacksmith, "Do you know what you just said?" The blacksmith admitted that he had no idea what the words he said meant. The Dutchman told him that he had been speaking German and had just said, "Devil, if you make this horse stand still you may have my soul." The frightened blacksmith vowed he would never again say those words.

This story I now told to the doctor, but it didn't faze him a bit. He merely said coldly, "I know what I am doing." He again began to utter words, so low and fast that I couldn't see how they could come out without tumbling over each other. An awful feeling enveloped me, and I again pushed his hands away. "How do you know? Maybe you are invoking the powers of the devil," I said in fright.

The doctor was disgusted and said, "If I can make this big tumor that is killing you shrink away, what do you care of what power I use?" He again proceeded with his charm. And suddenly I knew! This was one of those witch doctors I had heard about. I hastily pushed his hands away again, sat up, then jumped off the table and ran out the door in a panic.

"Hey, come back here!" Shem cried. "What do you mean by running off like this?"

But I was out the door and gone already, running down the road. I would walk home, rather than stay a minute longer in that sinister room. I walked on and on until I became so faint with hunger and thirst that I stopped at a spring by the roadside for a cool, refreshing drink and to rest. It was then that I heard the clop of horses' hooves, and saw Shem and the wagon come round the bend.

"Get in the wagon, you crazy woman!" he yelled angrily. "You surely deserve to die for disobeying me. The tumor will keep right on growing and choke the breath out of you, and you surely deserve it for running off like that. You crazy fool!"

I shuddered, but made no reply. I wished I'd never been born and never had brought three innocent children into the world. As we silently plodded homeward, tears flowed down over my cheeks and dark clouds of dread and fear descended all around me. When we finally reached home I felt as bone weary and downcast as the horses looked. Shem reached under the wagon seat and pulled out a big potato and held it up.

"Now, listen carefully to what I have to say," he said sternly. "The doctor said you can still be healed if you follow his instructions closely. See this biggest eye here on the potato? You place this potato in a crock in the cellar with the eye facing toward the north when the moon is waxing, and turn it toward the south when the moon is waning, for three months. Also, turn it around three times completely, once every day, while chanting these words:

> *Earth and heaven,*
> *Heaven and earth,*
> *Birth and death,*
> *Death and birth."*

I took the potato, knowing he would make me do as he said, but resolved to turn it just the opposite way of what he'd said. I'd turn it toward the south when the moon was waxing, and toward the north when the moon was waning. And I wouldn't say the words, either. And that's what I've been doing since, Shem asks me every evening if I've turned the potato today. How thankful I am that he doesn't ask me if I've chanted the rhyme, or if I've turned the potato in the right direction!

Here's my hymn for today:

> *All hail the power of Jesus' name!*
> *Let angels prostrate fall.*
> *Bring forth the royal diadem,*
> *And crown Him Lord of all.*

September—The leaves are starting to fall from the trees, and we've had some clear blue-sky weather, sure signs that fall is approaching. My heart is very heavy these days, for we've been stunned with the news that a sudden sickness, probably cholera, has hit the Alden family and spared only the father, Jotham. Oh, how can I bear to even write this, that dear Opal and all her little ones have gone and joined the two firstborn in the family in the graveyard on the hill. I hadn't seen Opal for over three months, and I've missed her so, and now I'll never see her again in this vale of tears. Poor Jotham! How utterly alone he must feel.

For a few fleeting moments I entertained the thought that if I had heeded Jotham's advice I would still be a widow now, and perhaps eventually he would ask me to be his wife, and I'd have a Christian home for my children. But then I remembered the tumor that is slowly ebbing away my life, and that is when the terrible thought hit me. Who would take my children, now that Opal is gone? And I cried bitter tears, and my heart aches fiercely ever since. Oh, what will become of my children?

The growth is getting bigger and bigger and sometimes I can feel it beginning to choke me a bit, especially when I draw a deep breath or cough. Sometimes I awaken in a panic at night, feeling the ruthless hands of death choking the life out of me. And then when I finally drop off to sleep, I dream that Shem is whipping Josiah and Abigail and they're screaming for mercy. Sometimes I wonder, would it have been all right to let the witch doctor try to remove the tumor? But when daylight comes, I know I made the right decision, and I'll keep on turning the potato in the wrong direction and I'll pray to God without ceasing.

The Bible verse for today:

October—We've had a busy summer and fall. Our large garden patch did very well and I am so pleased and thankful. It produced a bounteous harvest of onions, beans and corn, which we dried; carrots, beets, and turnips, which we stored in the root cellar. We've also just finished cooking our winter's supply of apple butter. Life goes on even when one's heart is breaking, I've found, and now I'm feeling new rays of hope once more.

The peddler man came around again in his rattly old wagon and when he displayed his wares, I spied my old Bible along with his other things! I grabbed it up and clasped it to my breast, with tears streaming down over my face. The peddler is a sweet old man, and when he saw how much the Bible had meant to me, and perceived that selling it had not been my idea, he told me I could have it back again. Oh, how very kind of him!

I told him that I am dying from this tumor on my neck and how I needed the word of God in this time of trial. He looked at me closely for a moment, then said, "I don't know lady, but that round swelling on your neck looks to me a lot like a goiter."

I stared at him uncomprehendingly for a long moment and asked, "What's a goiter?"

He replied, "I don't rightly know myself, lady, but I do know that sometimes it's cured by getting more iodine in your diet. There are some kinds of fish that contain a lot of iodine, in fact, I have a crate of such fish along right now. It's dried ocean fish that are rich in iodine, and if you eat one of these every day, you might be cured. It'd be worth a try."

It sounded unbelievable, but still, it caused a ray of hope to spring unbidden into my heart. Oh, how I longed to buy those dried fish. But I sadly shook my head. "I haven't a cent of money in the house," I said. "I can't buy them."

"That's a pity," the peddler said regretfully. "I'm sorry I can't give them to you like I gave the Bible, for they cost me a pretty penny. There ought to be someway though, that you could have those fish. Is there anything you could trade for them?"

I went back into the house, trying to think of what we would have that we don't really need. Was there any such thing in the entire house? My eyes lighted on the lovely glass vase on the mantle, which belonged to Shem's first wife. Would he mind if I traded it? I decided to risk it.

"Good enough," the peddler said happily. "I knew there had to be a way." He lifted the crate of fish out of the wagon, with instructions to soak each fish in water overnight, then cook it the next day, long enough for the bones to soften so that they can be eaten, too. With a wave of his hand he drove off, wishing me a fast recovery.

I hid the box of fish in the *kammerli* (little closet) up in the loft, and now I'll see what happens. I've put one out to soak for tomorrow. Thankfully, they're little fish. I don't think I could manage to eat a big fish by myself in a day's time. And I'll still keep turning the potato the wrong way.

Time for a hymn:

> *Come let us tune our loftiest song,*
> *And raise to Christ our joyful strain;*
> *Worship and thanks to Him belong,*
> *Who reigns and shall forever reign.*

> *Extol the lamb with loftiest song,*
> *Ascend to Him our cheerful strain;*
> *Worship and thanks to Him belong,*
> *Who reigns and shall forever reign.*

October 16—When Shem came in late last night in a half-drunken state, he noticed right away that the vase was no longer on the mantle and angrily demanded to know what had happened to it. I tried to stay calm as I told him I traded it for things I needed off the peddler wagon. I cringed as Shem's bloodshot eyes and puffy face became distorted with anger. With a roar of fury he lunged for me, but tripped over a block of firewood and fell sprawling on the floor. I ran for the door, out into the cool night air, and ran into the shadowy darkness of the woods.

Shem did not follow me, and so I sat on a fallen log, watching the doorway. At last I saw him come out and go to the stable. He came back out with a saddle horse, mounted it and rode away off into the darkness. I returned to the house, lit a candle and now I'm sitting on the doorstep, waiting for his return. He will probably be too drunk to be very dangerous when he gets back. Perhaps his cronies will bring him back stoned, like they once did. By tomorrow, he may have forgotten his rage. Oh, the terrible evils of liquor!

Oh, Lord, what will become of my little ones? Oh, take them home to Yourself when I die, safe in the Heavenly mansions over yonder.

"Though He slay me, yet will I trust in Him: But I will maintain mine own ways before Him. He also shall be my salvation: For an hypocrite shall not come before Him."

November 2—What a succession of weary days these past few weeks have been. As I had written in my last journal entry, that Shem's cronies may perhaps bring him home, so it came to pass. They brought him home, lifeless and still, killed in a drunken brawl. They buried him the next day, without any scripture reading or ceremony of any kind. My heart feels numb and dazed. What will become all of us now? I know I am dying and what will become of these nine orphans in my care? I've been continuing to cook and eat the peddler's fish everyday, but it's not helping a bit, My tumor or goiter seems to be as large as ever, maybe even growing a little bit larger. Oh, my poor, poor children. I threw out the potato in the cellar, thankful to be rid of it. I know I'm dying, it's just a matter of time now.

November 7—We have visitors. Shem's sister Selie and her husband, Morse, came this morning and are taking over here. They're claiming this place, house and all, and telling me I'll have to leave. They're childless and say they want to raise Shem's children as their own, but have enough without my three yet.

I told them I have no place to go, but they have that all figured out already, too. Morse has two bachelor brothers who live together in a four-room house 18 miles west of here and have two extra rooms they'll rent out to me, in exchange for me doing the cooking. They're coming tomorrow morning, with their horses and wagon to take me and the children to their home. Selie said there's room for a large garden at their place, and the bachelors will see to it that there's provisions for the table. Yes, it doesn't sound like the most ideal set-up, but what else can I do? I hope and pray that it will be all right and that I can provide a Christian environment for the children.

I know it's not right what Selie and Morse are doing for part of Shem's inheritance would rightfully belong to me. Yet what can I say, they're forcing me to get out. Morse told me I must sign a paper that says the farm goes to him and Selie, which is fair enough if they're raising and providing for Shem's children, and that's final. Sighs.

There was no love in our marriage and I have no regrets of parting with Shem, but still, it's turning my world even more upside down. Will there ever be peace and contentment and happiness in my life? It's all a vale of tears and sorrow. If only I had listened to Jotham and Opal when they warned me.

A Bible verse for today:

"O, that I had the wings of a dove that I might fly away and be at rest." (Psalms)

December 5—How drastically my life has changed in these past few weeks. Sometimes I wonder if I'm just dreaming and will wake up to harsh realities again. The day after my last journal entry I got Josiah, Abigail, and Aimee ready and packed our clothes into a knapsack, then tearfully kissed little Callie goodbye, for she had become very dear to me and I knew I'd miss her sorely. The boys, too, had begun to seem like my own, and it wrenched at my heart to leave them with Selie and Morse. But the bachelor brothers' wagon was coming and there was nothing I could do but hug them goodbye and climb aboard.

Before we had gone many miles, I could soon tell that those two men were not what Selie had made them out to be and I perceived that they had no honorable intentions. With growing alarm I wondered what I should do for I had no other place to go. I prayed to God for help and He intervened. At the junction in the road, where the brothers were intending to head west, a wheel broke off the wagon and we were delayed until they fixed it. That is when I made up my mind that we would part company with the bachelors and strike out on our own.

We were just around five miles from the cabin where George and I had been so happy together and perhaps no one was occupying it now and the children and I could find shelter there. Anything would be better than going with those men and what they had in mind. They sat by the roadside eating the provisions they'd packed and though the children stood watching hungrily, they offered them none. Soon they were snoozing and so I quietly gathered the children and my knapsack and we headed down the path. I hoped to be far away by the time they awoke.

Thankful that it was a mild Indian summer day, we trudged onward, as fast as I dared make the children walk. At the next crossing, kind Providence sent help in the form of a man and woman on a spring wagon hitched with a high-stepping horse. They offered us a ride and tears of thankfulness slid down over my cheeks. What a relief to know that we would be safely out of the reach of the bachelors. The couple were on their way to Rock Springs and were going right by the road that led to George's cabin, our old home. In a very short time, we were dropped off at the corner, not even a mile from our old place.

Eagerly we walked the short distance, but, alas, when we rounded the bend and saw our homestead, there was the sound of children's voices as they played in the yard, and a plump woman sat on the doorstep holding a baby (where I myself had so often sat).

With a tear and a sigh, we sank down on a fallen log by the roadside, with the children whimpering that they were thirsty and tired. I was bone-weary myself, more from the strain rather than much walking. I knew that down the road aways there was a spring bubbling out of the ground not ten feet from the trail. There we quenched our thirst with the clear, sparkling water and then sat to rest by the spring pool. I was exceedingly worried. What would we do? Where would we go? I thought of Hagar and her son, there in the wilderness long ago, and how she had lifted up her voice and wept, and God had opened her eyes and she saw a well of water and she filled her water bottle and gave some to the lad. Would God provide for us, too?

The children were crying from hunger, all three of them, and I wanted to cry, too. Suddenly, I remembered the loaf of bread I had put into the knapsack with the clothes. With a grateful heart I got the loaf and with heartfelt thanks to God for it, I broke it into pieces for the children. This brought smiles to their faces and after we had eaten, we all felt better. We all had a nap and by that time I had made up my mind . . . I had the children to think of, and so I'd swallow my pride and go to Jotham Alden for help. Somehow we made it, walking several weary miles, with me carrying little Aimee often, and then about a mile from Jotham's homestead we heard a horse and wagon coming from behind. It was Jotham, and at the sight of him my legs suddenly threatened to give way. What, oh what, would I say to him?

"Whoa!" he said to his horse and jumped to the ground. "Well, well, what a surprise to find you all here," he said with a smile lighting his face. "Climb aboard and I'll give you a lift to wherever you're going."

Wherever you're going. His words reminded me of the stark reality that we had no place to go and I suddenly and helplessly burst into unwelcome tears. I had been planning what I would say to him, but now I could not even speak. Jotham calmly lifted the children into the wagon, and bade me to climb in too, then wordlessly drove on, perceiving that we were in trouble.

At his barn he tied the horse and invited us to come inside. By the aroma I could tell there was a pot of beans simmering on the hearth and a plate of biscuits graced the table. The kitchen was clean, homey and inviting, but the thought that cheerful, kindhearted Opal was not there and would never come back, brought on a fresh flood of tears, and I sank down on Opal's rocker. Jotham brought out brightly dressed rag dolls for the girls to play with and a wooden horse and wagon for Josiah.

By that time I had regained my composure and swallowing my pride once more, I told Jotham of our sad plight, and that I was dying and worrying so about what would become of the children after I'm gone. I told him what the peddler man had said about the fish, but that they hadn't helped at all and that I was so tired, so weary and discouraged. I told him I never wanted to get married again, but I wanted a home and a Christian father for my children after I'm gone and I was wondering if he'd be willing to be that to them.

Jotham looked exceedingly troubled after I had spoken my piece. He talked about how it's only been a few months since Opal passed away and that he's not planning to ever re-marry, but he sees the dire straits we're in. He said that he would give us a home if it would be proper, which it wouldn't, unless we'd go through a marriage ceremony. After talking for an hour, we agreed on such an arrangement. We ate supper while it was still daylight, then Jotham hitched two fresh horses to the wagon and we set out for Rock Springs. We figured we would arrive in time to hunt up the parson to have the ceremony performed and then spend the night at the inn and come home the next morning. I'll have to finish this later, for it's time to go milk the cow and then cook a kettleful of cornmeal mush for frying for breakfast. I'll take time to copy a hymn first:

Hark the glad sound, the Savior comes,
The Savior promised long.
Let every heart prepare a throne,
And every voice a song.

Our glad hosannas, Prince of Peace,
Thy welcome shall proclaim.
And Heaven's eternal arches ring,
With Thy beloved name.

December 6—While Aimee and Abigail nap, and Josiah is outside with Jotham, I'll try to write the rest of our adventure. With the buffalo robes, we made nests on the back of the wagon for the children then started out on the 20 mile trek to Rock Springs. All sorts of emotions chased each other through my mind, first self-berating and condemnation, then gratitude and thankfulness, then doubts and fears again, until I became too confused to think at all. The road seemed long and bumpy, and Jotham and I exchanged few words, but the children chattered excitedly from the back of the wagon. At least they enjoyed the ride.

At last we saw the lights of the town up ahead, and Jotham remarked that he hoped the parson hadn't gone gallivanting to another part of the country to hold revival meetings. We stopped at the Warden Inn first, and secured a room for the night, for the children and me. Jotham said he would sleep on the wagon. There we learned that the parson was indeed in town, at his sister's place just across the road from the inn. Jotham went over immediately and talked to the preacher (the same one who had married Shem and me) who agreed to perform the ceremony at his sister's house at 8 o'clock for a fee. It seemed awfully high, but it surely is worth a lot to the children and I, having the security of a Christian father and home.

Shortly before 8:00, we put the children to bed, the girls in the big bed where I would join them later, and Josiah on the cot in the corner. Then we set out together, walking across the street to the parson to be married. I thought of what a joyous occasion this could be if it were for a real marriage, but cast the thought aside, feeling thankful for what I had and what it would mean to the children. I knew that Jotham would never let us down, and that he's entirely trustworthy and would do right by us.

As we left the street, Jotham led the way up the steps to the yard, unexpectedly a small black and white creature scampered out of the bushes and raised a tail in warning. Jotham quickly stepped back and held out his arm to stop me.

"A skunk," he whispered. "Step back to the street."

Both of us turned around to retreat, but it was too late. Skeet! And then we were drenched with the evil-smelling vapor. Coughing and choking, and with eyes a-watering, we ran back across the street to the inn. Thankfully, Mr. and Mrs. Warden came to our aid, giving us some of their clothing, blocks of lye soap, and towels and told us to go down to the creek at the back of the inn to wash.

Jotham went pieceways upcreek to a grove of trees to shed his clothes and I went as far downstream. We were having a spell of mild Indian summer weather just then, but still, the creek water was very chilly! Into it I plunged, scrubbing away for all I was worth with that strong lye soap, until I was numb, and blue with cold, and my teeth were chattering. I left my smelly clothes lay, donned Mrs. Warden's clean things, then dashed back to the inn. Mrs. Warden kindly let me in to warm myself by the fire, and gave me a mug of hot tea. Jotham was already there, looking as if he were a little amused. By the twitching of his lips, I knew he wanted to laugh. And then we tried it again, going across the street to be married, and this time made it safely.

The parson, upon hearing of our misfortune, said he would step outside to tie the knot, and he made sure he didn't stand too close. We had no witnesses but the parson assured us it would be all right in this case. As soon as he had pronounced us man and wife, he disappeared back into the house. We crossed back over the street to the inn and I crept upstairs to my sleeping babes, hoping I wouldn't disturb them, and that they wouldn't catch a whiff of skunk. Jotham slept in the barn, under the buffalo robes on the wagon. If anyone had noticed, and wondered why we didn't room together, we would have had a good excuse.

It's a wonder we didn't both catch a good dose of pneumonia from bathing in the cold creek water, but thankfully God protected us from even as much as catching a cold. I'm beginning to feel at home here in Jotham's house and the children love it. They have a much more wholesome and peaceful environment now, where they aren't subject to Shem's rages.

I find myself wishing I could now live for a long time, and find it hard to bear that my days are numbered. Will Jotham be able to be a father and mother both to the children after I'm gone? I'm praying that God will give me a year or two here with them before I must leave.

Bible verse for today:

"Truly my soul waiteth upon God: From Him cometh my salvation. He only is my rock and my salvation; He is my deference; I shall not be greatly moved."

<u>Part Four</u>

Sunshine and Lamplight

December 8—When I awoke this morning, for a moment I forgot where I was. I'd had a dream of George and the days when we were so happy together. And then, by the light of the sun shining in the window, I saw the high-boy and the clothes tree, and I remembered that this was Opal's room, Opal's and Jotham's, and that I was a stranger in the house, an intruder, a beggar, and an imposter and I wanted to cry.

I heard Jotham stirring around in the lean-to, then going out to the kitchen. He brought in a load of firewood, for I heard him dropping it on the hearth. I still didn't get up; for a moment I wished I'd never have to get up again. But then I remembered the children and quickly jumped out of bed. By then the aroma of boiling coffee filled the house.

When I entered the kitchen, Jotham was standing by the hearth, his head resting on his arm against the mantle. Hearing me coming into the room, he lifted his head, and I saw a flicker of pain in his eyes. But he forced a smile and said pleasantly, "Good morning, Julia." This must be awfully hard for him, having me step into Opal's shoes so soon after her passing. How my heart aches for him. I can't imagine bearing what he had to go through, losing Opal and all the children, all in a few day's time. Would I ever recover from such a shock?

I was stirring the batter for the pancakes when the children came pattering into the kitchen, chattering brightly. They're the ray of sunshine in this home, and Jotham seems to appreciate them, too. Maybe with their innocent cheerfulness they'll ease the pain of losing his own children.

Jotham spent the day in the woodshed. He's working at making another bedstead and chest of drawers for himself to keep in the lean-to, so he won't have to sleep on the floor and will have room for his clothes. Josiah was with him all day for Jotham is his hero, and I'm so thankful for his influence over my boy. Imagine Shem being anyone's hero. Thank God, Josiah will have a Christian example of manhood to pattern his life after.

The girls and I were making noodles today, and after they tired of helping, they were playing with their dolls on the pretty, round braided rug in front of the hearth. Opal made it herself, for I remember her telling me about it when she had her quilting. She made the coverlet for the rocker too, and the pretty quilt on "my" bed. Her presence is still in this home and I'm glad for it. She was such a special person. Someday we'll understand the pain and heartaches of our lives, and the purpose of it, but for now we see through a glass darkly.

Bible verse for today:

"I will lift mine eyes unto the hills, from whence cometh my help. My help cometh from the Lord, which made heaven and earth. He will not suffer thy foot to be moved; he that keepeth thee will not slumber." (Psalm 121:1-3)

December 13—Snow! A real blizzard, almost like those we used to have in Pennsylvania! That which I had feared and dreaded so when I lived alone in the cabin in the woods with my babes, is nothing but a minor inconvenience with a man like Jotham here to take care of the stock. He was up early this morning and saddled his most reliable horse to go check on his cattle that he has overwintering outside. His friendly dog, Sport, cavorted after him in the snow. When Josiah awoke, he thought it was a catastrophe that Jotham and Sport left without him. He and Sport are best of friends, romping together whenever he's outside. Shem's dog was much too vicious for him to befriend.

When Jotham came in he was looking worried, for he saw panther tracks in the snow. The promising yearling heifer is in danger, so he and Mr. Kitzmiller want to try to trail it and shoot it. Inside, the children and I had a jovial day making taffy and molasses cakes and watching it snow. When the snow stopped we all bundled up and went for a refreshing romp behind the house. The girls and I made a snowman and Josiah built a little snowhouse. I saw Jotham come out of the stable and stand there watching us a bit wistfully for a few minutes, but then he came and joined our fun. He helped Jotham build a real snowhouse with a doorway and a window and even a roof. It warmed my heart to see him so light-hearted and jovial-like.

A hymn for today:

Jesus, the very thought of Thee,
With sweetness fills my breast,
But sweeter far Thy face to see,
And in Thy presence rest.

Oh, hope of every contrite heart!
Oh, joy of all the meek!
To those who fall, how kind Thou art!
How good to those who seek!

December 20—Christmas is in the air and the children are excited about it. They're hoping for gifts, but I want to make sure I instill in them the true meaning of Christmas.

Today the Kitzmillers came on the sleigh, all 13 of them, with the youngest baby only three months old, bundled up under the robes. They brought candies for the children, and cheer and joy for me. Mr. Kitzmiller spent the day hunting the panther with Jotham, and Mrs. Kitzmiller brought her knitting. She says their house is bursting at the seams and they're planning to build an addition, come spring. Her elderly parents live with them now too, and that takes an extra room.

She brought dried plums, so we made plum pudding and slow-roasted her stuffed pig stomachs along with it for dinner. What a delicious meal! After the dishes were washed, she got her brood to sing Christmas carols for us. The beauty of their childish voices ringing out clear and sweet brought tears to my eyes.

I wished every child could have a good home with kind, loving parents, and plenty to eat at this Christmas season.

The Kitzmillers left at mid-afternoon, but Jotham didn't come back until dark, after the children were already in bed. He looked very tired after walking for miles chasing the big cat without any success. But he brightened up when he saw the big portion of stuffed pig stomach and plum pudding that I had saved for him.

I sat at the table with him, talking about this and that, and watching him eat. After the meal he leaned back in his chair and told me all about their exciting day in the woods. They had come close to shooting the wildcat, but not close enough. Maybe next time. ,

Then he showed me the gifts he'd made for the children out in the woodshed when I thought he was working on the bedstead. There was a little doll cradle for the girls and a sled for Josiah. They'll be a happy bunch when they see these gifts. I'll make a soft little comforter for the cradle, and I've already made the girls each a new rag doll. For Josiah, I made a stuffed riding horse on a stick. We are truly blessed, with so much to be thankful for.

After Jotham had gone to bed, I stood at the window, watching the moon rise over the snowy landscape and shining down through the bare trees. It was a beautiful, calm, and silent night, with silvery moonlight transforming everything into a thing of beauty.

Bible verse for today:

"And suddenly there was with the angel a multitude of the heavenly host praising God and saying, "Glory to God in the highest, and on earth, peace, goodwill toward men." (Luke 2:13-14)

January 17—After a week of mild, balmy weather, winter's winds and snow flurries are back again. I've been wondering so much how my boys and little Callie are making out with Selie and Morse. I guess I must've mentioned something to Jotham about it, for today, after he had finished the morning chores, he hitched the horses to the wagon and told me to get ready. We're going back to visit Shem's family. What a nice surprise! Josiah was all excited about it, too, for he missed Jan a lot, and Abigail was delighted to go see Callie again.

It wasn't until we were bundled up and on our way, with the children snuggled under the robes on the back of the wagon, that Jotham told me what was on his mind. He wanted to bring back that box of fish that I had gotten from the peddler. He said that he has a good bit of faith in the man's knowledge, and that there's logic in what he said. He thinks those fish would help me. Oh, what a glad feeling it gave me to know that Jotham hoped I'd recover. He's so kind and thoughtful to us, the intruders in his home and the disturbers of his peace, in all probability.

The ride was a chilly one, and I was glad when we reached Shem's place, although I didn't know how we'd be received. Trix bounded out to meet us, barking savagely, but soon his tail was awag, and I think he even smiled a bit. Next the boys and Callie came running, and

I hugged them all and grabbed up little Callie into the biggest hug of all. I do believe that Selie and Morse are doing right by Shem's children for they seem well and happy and the place has a neat appearance.

The boys informed me that Selie and Morse weren't at home, that they'd gone to town for supplies. And so I had a happy day with my former family. Rufe and Lars were pleased that I got dinner for the family so they wouldn't have to cook. Josiah and Jan had great fun, and

Abigail and Callie played like old times. I hope we'll be able to visit them often, and if I can't be a mother to them perhaps I can be like an aunt to them.

Mid-afternoon, just before it was time to leave I went up to the loft to the *kammerli* and found the crate of fish just like I'd left them and brought them downstairs. We explained to the boys why I needed them, then we bundled up again, said our goodbyes and headed for the wagon. Jotham was walking on ahead carrying the fish, when we heard a shout from the barn. Selie and Morse were home and Morse came over, looking a bit stern-faced and wanted to know what was in the crate. When he saw it was fish, he said we could gladly have them, but when Jotham offered to pay for them, he was happy to accept the offer. I guess there'd be a good bit of trouble if I'd try to claim anything of Shem's, but thankfully, there's no need for that.

A hymn for today:

> *Thou art the way; to Thee alone,*
> *From sin and death we flee . . .*
> *And he who would the Father see,*
> *Must seek Him, Lord, by Thee.*
>
> *Thou art the Truth; Thy word alone,*
> *True wisdom can impart . . .*
> *Thou only canst inform the mind,*
> *And purify the heart.*

February 4—Every morning after we're done with the morning meal, Jotham takes down the family Bible and reads aloud a portion of scripture, in that deep, rich voice of his. It makes me think back to that day that now seems so long ago, when I informed Opal and Jotham that I intended to accept Shem's offer of marriage, and Jotham also took down the Bible and read to me the verses about being unequally yoked together with unbelievers. I foolishly and willfully followed my own whims, disregarding his kind advice; and oh, how I suffered for it. I often wonder what the course of my life would have been had I heeded his advice. But God has been good to me, and delivered me from my folly, perhaps for the children's sake. They are very happy here. Josiah is out with Jotham constantly, and the girls love him too, for he always has a kind word for them. Sometimes I see him brushing away a tear and I know he's thinking of Opal and their children and of the days when they were a happy family together.

God moves in a mysterious way sometimes, to make His will known, and though His chastening may be grievous to us at times, it yields the peaceable fruits of righteousness. Someday we'll know and understand why we have to endure all these heartaches here on earth.

March 3—I heard a robin singing this morning, and now I know that spring is on the way! We've already had several meals of dandelion, and tonight I took my paring knife and headed for the big spring in the meadow to hunt for watercress. I found a big patch of it, and after I had cut enough for several meals, I sat on the big rock beside the pool to reminisce a bit.

There was a big oak tree growing beside the pool and it brought back memories of my days in the Conestoga Valley of Pennsylvania where I had a favorite retreat on a rock under a big oak tree. I thought of Bright Wings, the Indian maiden; lively, outgoing Hannah; and the Wittman family I worked for. I wondered about Abe and Margaret Rittenhouse, how many children they had, and where they lived by now. It's hard telling what my life might have been like had I gotten my way for I was so determined to win Abe's heart. Perhaps I wouldn't have needed to suffer so, both in losing George and in my marriage with Shem. But all things work together for good, to them that love God and are called according to His purpose.

I have many blessings and I feel at peace with the thought that the children will be well taken care of when I'm gone. It's heartwarming to me that Jotham makes sure I cook and eat one of the ocean fish every day. I do believe he's anxious for me to recover. But, of course, I guess he is, for how could he manage alone with both the children and the farm to care for, if I weren't here?

I started my spring housecleaning today, and what fun it was to clean and air the rooms. This house isn't as big as Shem's was, but it's newer and I like it better. There are two pine trees in the front yard and the apple orchard out back. A stake-and-rider fence encircles the *shier-hof* (barnyard) and there's the big spring in the meadow. And I often like to go out to the barn, to pet the big horses and to hear their eager whinnies and nickers, and feel their friendly nuzzlings.

Tonight as I was caressing Daisy's silvery-maned neck, I turned around to see Jotham standing there with a certain undefinable expression on his face. He quickly turned and left the stable and I saw him head for the hill across the way to the rows of grave markers that stand sentinel over his buried hopes and dreams. As I watched, I saw Josiah and Abigail run after him, and then the three walked hand-in-hand together up the hill. Aimee came to me and grabbed my hand, begging for us to follow them, but I thought better of it. Perhaps he needed that time to be alone with his thoughts of his departed loved ones, that is, if Josiah and Abigail's chatter didn't distract him from it.

Ya well, it's time I should go and finish putting things back in the rooms I housecleaned. In the *kammerli* upstairs I found Opal's clothes and had to brush away a few tears myself, remembering her. She was such an unselfish, generous and thoughtful person, and I know I could never take her place.

A hymn for today:

O Savior, precious Savior,
Whom yet unseen we love!
O name of might and favor,
All other names above!

We worship Thee, we bless Thee,
To Thee, O Christ, we sing!
We praise Thee and confess Thee,
Where perfect praises ring!

March 22—Last night I was awakened from a deep sleep by a panther's scream in the distance. What a chilling, spine-tingling cry it was, and I felt lonely and forlorn. I heard Jotham stirring in the lean-to, so I knew he'd heard it, too. Probably the same one they were tracking last fall and never caught. There's going to be a new little calf after awhile and I hope it will be protected from the beast.

We had some excitement this forenoon, too, when Jotham was plowing in the south field. I was making biscuits and the little girls were mixing the dough when we heard shouts of terror from Josiah. He had been following Jotham's plow, picking up earthworms to use when he went fishing when suddenly the ground gave way beneath the horses and they were floundering in the earth. Down to their bellies they sank and there they were stuck. A sink hole! That was when Josiah came running to the house, yelling frantically that the horses were half buried.

I suppose Jotham has had sink holes on the farm before, for he knew just what to do. He hitched the other two workhorses to the sunken ones, with ropes around their middles, and then slowly but surely heaved them out. The children and I sat on the fencerow watching, and rejoiced when they were free.

By that time the sky was darkening for a spring storm, and we hurried for the house. A flash of lightening filled the sky, thunder rumbled in the east, and I knew it was coming fast. The wind was rising and the tree branches were thrashing to and fro. By the time Jotham had the horses safely in the barn and had made it to the house, he was drenched to the skin, the rainwater dripped off his hair and clothes and collected in puddles on the floor. I sent Josiah into the lean-to with Jotham's clean clothes, hoping he would realize that it was worth something to him to have someone wash his clothes and cook his meals.

Later I was ashamed of my thoughts, for he kindly helped to set the table for dinner, and then was very nice about it when I remembered that I had used the last of the bread this morning and had forgotten to start a new batch of dough. He even offered to help knead it, and with those powerful punches the new bread turned out extra light. He then put a new shelf in the pantry for my extra pots and pans that he had heard me wishing for. After that he gathered the children around him and told them stories, real interesting ones, even to me.

By mid-afternoon the rain was over and the sun shone warmly on the clean-washed earth. Jotham went back to his outdoor work, first gathering stones to fill up the sink hole. I hope spring's here to stay and the early flowers will soon be a-bloom and the redbuds, dogwoods, mountain laurel, and fruit trees at their nicest.

"For lo, the winter is past, the rain is over and gone, the flowers appear on the earth; the time of the singing of the birds is com,e and the voice of the turtledove is heard in our land."

April 4—The buds are coming out on the trees and the grass is greening. This morning as I went for a bucket of water down at the spring I found a circle of lovely bluebells in a little hollow, sweet and dew-covered. Next will be the violets and other woodland flowers. Oh, the beauties of springtime!

As I knelt for the water, I saw my reflection in the pool and saw the bulge where my goiter was, and my hand instinctively went to it. Did it seem to be a little smaller or did I just imagine it? I've been eating my fish faithfully, and I've been ever so hopeful lately, and praying daily.

I know that Jotham's praying, too, for he told me so himself the other evening when I met him at the *schier-hof* gate, after bringing up the cow. He wondered if I'm well enough to consider having church services here at our homestead next Sunday, and that's when he told me he was praying for me daily to be feeling well, and for the goiter to be receding. I told him that his prayers are being answered, for I'm feeling better than I have for a long time.

For a long while I had been feeling fidgety and anxious and my heartbeat fluttered so at times. I used to think it was from the trouble I was having in my marriage to Shem, but now I believe it was part of the condition that caused the goiter to grow in the first place. I had a good appetite, but only became thinner, and now that is changing for the better, too.

We agreed to announce it on Sunday at church that we'll have services here next time and that will make me very busy getting ready. Being able to go to church services again has been such a blessing to me. God is so good. He gave my Bible back to me and the blessings of Christian fellowship and a wholesome environment for the children. Praise God from whom all blessings flow. At church last Sunday it was said that there are still thieves in the area. The strange part about it is that the thieves often strike when the settlers are at church services or revival meetings. I hope they never come here again. Opal's chickens were already stolen once from here.

There is also a rumor noised abroad that there's a preacher and his family moving into the area soon. I do hope it is true. I asked Jotham why we don't get the same parson to preach for us Sundays who performed our marriage ceremony, and he said that he and the other men at our services don't feel that he's preaching quite sound doctrine. In some points he has it right, but in others they feel he's minimizing some important concepts. I never really felt that the parson seemed like a real preacher at all, but I know I shouldn't be judgmental.

A Bible verse for today:

> *"Let us hear the conclusion of the whole matter: Fear God and keep His commandments; for this is the whole duty of man. For God shall bring every work into judgement, with every secret thing, whether it be good or whether it be evil."*
> (Ecclesiastes 12:13, 14)

April 25—I feel like my health is improving rapidly, and the goiter has shrunk noticeably. Praise be! Preacher Barnes and his wife and seven children have arrived. They moved to Shem's homestead. What a shock it was for us to hear that Selie and Morse have moved the family to Virginia without saying a word to us beforehand. Perhaps they were afraid we'd insist on having a share of the sale of the farm, or, if it wasn't that, we'd lay claim to some or all of the children. I'll be praying for the boys and little Callie everyday, hoping they'll grow up to be fine Christians. I wish I could have done more for them, and be able to have some influence over their lives.

I'm sitting down here by the spring pool to write. Abigail and Aimee are with me, sitting on the rock playing with their dolls as they chatter away. Jotham and Josiah are planting corn in the east field. It's a beautiful evening for the frogs are chorusing poignantly, the whippoorwills are calling, the spring peepers are singing, and the gentle breezes are wafting delightful woodsy spring fragrances our way. My thoughts travel to the graveyard on the hill, and I wonder if it's true that it's always springtime in Heaven.

The children and I planted clumps of ferns, violets and forget-me-nots around the gravestones, and I wondered if Jotham noticed. He goes there often and sits, either meditating or praying for awhile, then when he comes back, he seems very quiet and pensive. I think perhaps he's still grieving much, and I pray for him daily. My memories of George are becoming fainter, and for Shem I haven't grieved at all.

Later, when Jotham and Josiah came in from the field they joined us by the spring pool to enjoy the beauties of the spring evening with us. Jotham was in a reminiscing mood and talked of his boyhood years of growing up on their farm in Massachusetts. Maybe someday we can travel back to Pennsylvania and then on to his homeplace, and visit dear ones back there. It's wishful thinking, I'm afraid, but it doesn't hurt to dream. It seems like ages since I've heard from Father and Mother Kettie, my brothers, or my sister Maria and her husband Rutherford and their boys. But I have memories of them, and I can remember them in my prayers.

Here is a hymn:

Oh, could I speak the matchless worth,
Oh, could I sound the glories forth,
Which in my Savior shine.

I'd soar and touch the heavenly strings,
And vie with Gabriel while he sings,
In tones almost divine.

May 10—Wildflowers are abundant everywhere and the earth is a green and beautiful place. I'm feeling so well, and the amazing part is, I hadn't realized how poorly I was actually feeling until I was better. Those fish must be working wonders or maybe it's all a miracle of God. Whatever it is, I'm very thankful I didn't allow that witch doctor to say his charms over me.

On Saturday evening we hitched up the two horses to the wagon and set out to visit Preacher Barnes and his family. They haven't been to services yet, for Mr. Barnes had hurt his leg and was laid up for a week or two. My, they're a friendly family! Mrs. Barnes is plump, jolly and bustling, and Mr. Barnes is very genial and good-hearted. The children take after their parents, too, and I'm sure they'll all be an asset to our community. That place brought back a lot of memories, things I'm trying to forget, but I'm afraid some of them will haunt me the rest of my days. I'll try to do as it says in the scriptures:

"Finally brethren, whatsoever things are true, whatsoever things are honest, whatsoever things are just, whatsoever things are pure, whatsoever things are lovely, whatsoever things are of good report, if there be any virtue, and if there be any praise, think on these things."

June 14—The wild roses in the thickets and wayside are blooming and the strawberries on the hillside are ripe and sweet. Strawberry preserves sweetened with honey on fresh bread and newly-churned butter are simply delicious. This morning when I went to bring up the cows I discovered that the dry cow had presented us with a darling wobbly little calf. And a week ago, Judy, the mare, gave birth to a spindly, long-legged filly. Jotham was quite pleased with it, and jovially said that Josiah

should name it. They're together constantly, and I do declare , I'm becoming just a wee bit jealous. (Smiles) Josiah chose the name Rosie for the filly, for it came into the world beside a blooming rose hedge.

And oh! I didn't write the best part of last week yet. Tuesday was my birthday and in the morning after chores, Jotham hitched the horses to the wagon and asked me to pack them some dinner (for him and Josiah). Josiah was all excited, and his twinkling hazel eyes reminded me so much of George's that I had to swallow a lump in my throat and brush away a few tears. He gleefully informed me that he and Jotham were going to Rock Springs and that I wasn't allowed to go along for they were going to choose a birthday gift for me. What pleasant flutterings of heart that gave me, and all day as the girls and I went about our work and play, I marveled at Jotham's thoughtful ways, and wondered what he would bring home.

We were busy in the garden all day, hoeing and weeding and picking hull peas and then shelling them. At last, just before supper was ready, the excited girls happily announced they saw the men returning, and ran out to meet the wagon, I had made a few extras for supper—the fresh peas, fresh lettuce from the garden, a strawberry shortcake, and freshly baked bread.

Josiah was all smiles as he proudly came in carrying a big package, while the girls gleefully danced around him, shouting for me to hurry and open it. I waited until Jotham came in, and then, with the children's eager help, tore off the wrappings. I gasped when I saw what it was, just what I'd always wished for, a lovely new lamp!

Jotham was smiling broadly at the children's eagerness and my obvious delight. After he had lit it with a twig of fire from the hearth it was even more beautiful and shed a rosy glow over the whole room. I placed the lamp on the mantle above the hearth, and our humble kitchen seemed transformed! And now I'll be able to see better to do hand sewing on the rocker by the hearthduring winter evenings. Dear, kind Jotham! I wonder what I could do for him when his birthday comes around.

After we'd eaten our supper they had a surprise for the girls, a stick of hard candy for each of them and one for Josiah, too. Jotham and I sat on the back stoop after the work was done and watched as the children played happily in the grass, while the fireflies flickered among the trees and thickets. We began counting our blessings and all we have to be thankful for—good health, plenty to eat and wear, friends, a preacher for our services, and even the Indians appear to be peaceable and friendly just now. A coppery moon rose up over the treetops, whippoorwills called to each other, and the night insects chorused. We are definitely blessed with peace, plenty of provisions for the cooking kettle on the hearth, and now even a lamp for shedding light on the hearth.

Time for a hymn:

> *Majestic sweetness sits enthroned,*
> *Upon the Savior's brow;*
> *His head with radiant glories crowned,*
> *His lips with grace o'erflow.*
>
> *Since from His bounty I receive,*
> *Such proofs of love divine;*
> *Had I a thousand hearts to give,*
> *Lord, they should all be Thine.*

August—Two months have passed since my last journal entry and they've been busy and comfortable. We've had abundant rainfall, and the corn has grown green and lush and tall. Of course, there are many weeds to be hoed, day after day. The morning glories twining up the cabin walls are blooming in profusion, and the wild daisies bordering the lane are at their prettiest.

This forenoon as I was hoeing the bean rows in the garden, I thought about how this has been our home now for nearly three-fourths of a year, and how my goiter has shrunk to almost nothing. How my heart rejoices, and yet I blush in shame for having thrown myself upon Jotham's mercy, telling him that I was dying. What else could he have done but give us a home, and to the children, his fathering. I wonder if he regrets it much, or just how he really feels. He's always wondrously kind, and disciplining the youngsters seems to come naturally to him. I suppose he's had a lot of experience, but still it's a marvel to me. He never punishes in anger, always lovingly but firmly, and the children love and respect him. How different from Shem's angry cuffings, ear boxings, and whippings, that brought a defiant, sullen and rebellious spark to the boys' eyes. I sure hope Selie and Morse will be able to do better by them.

Ya well, I must get busy, for there's heaps and heaps of corn to be cut from the cob and dried outside in the hot sunshine. There are beans to be picked and dried, and *hollerbier* (elderberries) to be picked and made into juice and pies.

Bible verse for today:

"Choose you this day whom ye will serve, as for me and my house, we will serve the Lord." (Joshua 24:15)

September 29—What a surprise we had today when a wagon with two horses hitched pulled into the *schierhof.* A bonneted woman sat on the seat beside a tall man, and try as I might, I couldn't make out who they were. The man tied his horses, then helped the woman down, and together they walked toward the house. I went to the door to welcome them, still not knowing who they were.

"Don't you know me anymore, Julia?" the smiling man asked, with a twinkle of amusement in his eyes. "I'm your cousin, Malcolm."

And then, with a flash of recognition, it all fell into place. He was Uncle Jeem's boy from Pennsylvania! Uncle Jeems was the one who had lost his leg years ago.

"This is my wife, Adah," he said. "We've come to Kentucky just last week, along with my sister Mary and her husband and children. They're in Rock Springs now."

"Mary!" I cried. "You mean they are in Kentucky right now?!" I was joyously astounded.

"Yes, and she sent us out here to find you and bring you to her for a visit. Since she arrived in Kentucky last week, she's been taken sick and can't travel for awhile."

Oh, my, so many questions I had to ask about the friends back home in the Conestoga Valley in Pennsylvania! Malcolm answered them the best he could.

Aunt Tilda is well, and Uncle Jeem's family is well, but Granny Magdalena has passed on to her reward. Abe and Margaret have moved westward and cousin Reba is now married to a Mennonite man and living near Earltown. Of my own family, Father and Mother Kettie and all the rest, he knows very little about, for they are only step-cousins of his and live 100 miles away.

Malcolm and Adah will stay for the night and then tomorrow, the children and I will travel with them to Rock Springs to visit cousin Mary. Her husband, Boyd, is traveling further west to build a cabin for the family, while Mary and the four children are staying with an older couple (a distant relative of Boyd's) in Rock Springs until the new cabin is finished. Malcolm and Adah will bring me home again the day after tomorrow. They have been negotiating on a parcel of land in this area. I'm really excited about the trip tomorrow, and I am glad that Jotham gave his blessing on my going. He will have to find out again what it's like to keep house on his own until we get back. Perhaps he will be glad for a few days of peace and quiet.

The hymn for today:

> *How sweet the name of Jesus sounds,*
> *In a believer's ear!*
> *It soothes his sorrows, heals his wounds,*
> *And drives away his fears.*
>
> *It makes the wounded spirit whole,*
> *And calms the troubled breast;*
> *'Tis manna to the hungry soul,*
> *And to the weary, rest.*

September 30—Here we are at the house where cousin Mary and her children are staying. I brought my journal along mainly so that Jotham won't perchance find it and read it. (Smiles)

Mary is still the same smiling, pretty girl, looking not much older than when I last saw her. Her children are as dear and sweet as my own three, and they all enjoyed playing with each other. Since she has arrived here in Kentucky, she's learned that there will be an addition to the family next spring, and because of health reasons, can't travel for a few weeks. We talked a blue streak, going from one heart-to-heart chat to the next, never running out of things to say. I hadn't realized how much I'd longed to have just such chats with another woman until now.

The Pennsylvania relatives had not heard of George's passing until just last spring, and hadn't heard of my re-marrying. I'm glad they hadn't heard about Shem.

The owners of this house are a dear old couple, and they welcomed me as warmly as if I were their own daughter. Tomorrow we will return home with Malcolm and Adah, back to Jotham and my duties. I'm looking forward to getting back and seeing the welcoming light in his eyes. Jotham's place is "Home Sweet Home" to me now, be it ever so common, there's no place like home.

October 1—Much to my disappointment, our planned trip home never materialized, for last night Malcolm's one horse died, and now he has to replace it before we can go back. I'm afraid we'll soon be wearing out our welcome here, but Mary says she's ever so thankful we're staying longer. We've been quilting, baking, making doughnuts, and having more chats, and the children are having a glorious time. So I guess I'll relax and enjoy my vacation. I have to wonder what Jotham's thinking, about why we didn't show up . . . is he worried?

A Bible verse for today:

"The Lord is my shepherd, I shall not want. He maketh me to lie down in green pastures. . . . He restoreth my soul."

October 3—We're still in Rock Springs, and I'm very eager to get home. The deal that Malcolm had with a horse dealer fell through at the last minute and now we're stranded. Last night I spent some sleepless hours and it was then in searching my soul that I came to the realization that I love Jotham and never want to be separated from him again. I cried into my pillow for awhile, but then I lit a candle and read a few chapters of scripture and felt comforted again. Even if he will never love me, I'll rejoice in being able to do things for him, and to make life as easy for him as possible.

"And He said unto me: My grace is sufficient for thee: For my strength is made perfect in weakness: Most gladly will I therefore rather glory in mine infirmities, that the power of Christ may rest upon me." (II Corinthians 12:9)

October 5—I'm home again, and happy as a lark! Feeling restless this morning at another day's delay in Rock Springs, I went for an early morning walk while the children were still sleeping. The frost was white on the fields outside of town, and the corn shocks and piles of pumpkins made it seem very autumn-like. Down the road aways I spied a two-horse wagon coming and the closer it came, the dearer the lone occupant on the seat looked. Yes . . . it *was* Jotham! I ran to meet him and climbed up on the seat beside him, so very glad to see him and his smile, but suddenly felt completely tongue-tied.

"Are you ready to come back?" he asked.

"More than ready!" I replied. "This has been too long."

"Awfully long and lonely," he agreed. "I'll think twice before I'll give you permission to go visiting without me again."

After I explained the delay to him, I asked, "What time did you start out to come here? In the middle of the night?"

"I won't say," Jotham replied, with a chuckle. His eyes twinkled, and he added, "We'll just say 'early.' After dinner the horses should be rested enough to start for home again."

We unhitched the horses and put them into the barn, then I ran to the house and got the children up, knowing they'd be delighted to see Jotham, too. They were so excited and climbed and romped all over him as he sat on the Boston rocker. I believe he was as glad to see them as they were to see him.

Jotham and I did some shopping together at the General Store in town, and at the Mercantile, and then I helped prepare the dinner and washed the dishes. Then we said our goodbyes and finally were on our way home.

When I'd left home, I had never thought it would be nearly a week until I'd be homeward bound again. The children snuggled under the buffalo robes on the back of the wagon, and Jotham and I mostly sat in comfortable silence, not saying much. The horses plodded onward, the wheels creaked round and round as the miles were covered. Suddenly I sat up straight.

"Jotham!" I cried. "You missed your road." We were headed for Shem's old place and I wondered why.

"Yes," Jotham said, smiling mysteriously. "We're going to see Preacher Barnes."

"But we just did visit them," I exclaimed, for our last church services had been at the Barnes' home.

Without replying, Jotham, with eyes a-twinkling, turned in at the Barnes' homestead, and stopped the horses in front of the barn. Turning to me, he said, "Julia, do you want to get married?"

"What!" I gasped. "I thought we were . . . uh . . . I mean..."

Jotham shook his head. "No, I guess we're not. I've just learned, while I was at Rock Springs, that the parson who performed the ceremony for our marriage really was no preacher, but was an imposter. He pretended to be one, but actually, he was part of a gang of thieves. While he was holding revival meetings and Sunday preachings, he sent out his cronies to rob the settlers that attended his gatherings. He went from town to town, doing his hypocrite's work for several years before he was caught. He will be put in the stocks and on the whipping post and locked up for a long time. So I'm asking you again, will you marry me?"

And of course, my answer was "yes" and given without a moment's hesitation. I was gloriously happy. Preacher Barnes couldn't hide the twinkle of amusement in his eyes when we stated our reason for coming, but he gladly performed the ceremony, and gave his hearty blessing on our vows as we plighted our hands in a union that would last until death parted us.

Mrs. Barnes invited us to stay for supper, and to us, it tasted as good as any grand wedding feast. There was joy and happiness, laughter and gaity aplenty and that makes even the most meager meal taste heavenly. After the supper dishes were washed, we all piled back on the wagon and headed for "Home Sweet Home." By then the stars were twinkling in the sky, and the night air was crisp and clean-smelling. Snuggled under the buffalo robes, the children fell asleep before we reached home, and Jotham carried them to their beds without awakening them. He's still out in the barn choring. I tidied up the kitchen and washed the dishes that Jotham had left from his morning meal, then resolved to fill the last pages in my journal and lay it away for good. There's room for one more hymn, and then it's farewell.

> *Thou hidden source of calm repose,*
> *Thou all-sufficient love divine,*
> *My help and refuge from my foes,*
> *Secure I am while Thou art mine;*
> *And lo! From sin and grief and shame,*
> *I hide me, Jesus, in Thy name.*

Thy mighty name salvation is,
And keeps my happy soul above,
Comfort it brings and power and peace,
And joy, and everlasting love;
To me, with Thy great name are given,
Pardon, and holiness and heaven.

— End of Julia's Journal —

February

Ya well, I've finally finished copying Julia's journal, over a year after I began and it ended at the best part. I suppose they lived happily ever after, like they do in storybooks. But I'm sure they had a lot of sad sorrowful times, too, for inside the back cover of her copybook, was this inscription:

A NOTE FROM ONE OF
JULIA'S GRANDDAUGHTERS

Jotham and Julia had six more children, but none of them lived to grow up. Three died as infants, and three died before they ever saw the light of day. And so the little graveyard on the hill has another row of little markers, beside Opal's and Jotham's (who lived to be 79 years old). When Josiah took a wife, he took over the Alden homestead and Jotham, Julia, and the girls moved to the Glauner homestead, into the cabin George had built for his family. It was there, under the eaves, or rafters, that the old journal was found years later. Julia lived to be 84 years old, and is buried beside her first husband, George. On her gravestone are inscribed these words: JULIA, Beloved wife of George Glauner and Jotham Alden. Nothing is said about Shem, for since the parson was a false one, she was never legally married to him. At the time of her death, Julia had 17 grandchildren and 43 great-grandchildren. She was a great blessing to her descendants.

It's been several weeks since I've finished copying Julia's journal, but I haven't gotten around to filling the last few pages of my own journal. Oh well, I suppose I have a good excuse, for a week ago today we became the parents of our adorable twins, babies Hiram Joel and Heidi Joy. They've been very brauf (good) so far, and we have a very capable helper in dear friend Sadie! And so together we've been enjoying the babies. Sadie says it's like playing dolls, only better. Kermit is as thrilled as I am, but we know it's a big responsibility to lead these precious souls in the paths of uprightness.

Heidi is blond and blue-eyed, and Hiram has dark hair. They don't look a bit alike, but are equally sweet. Right now, both are sleeping peacefully in the cradle. They fit in well now, but I suppose we'll soon have to get another cradle. Hannah and Henry love the babies dearly, and never seem to tire of holding them. I suppose they'll soon both be awake and chewing their fists, and Kermit will be in from the barn, and Hannah and Henry will be ready for their bedtime stories. Aunt Miriam sent me a letter and a poem, "Take Time with Your Children,"and perhaps I can copy it here in my journal sometime, in order to fill the last pages and to remind me that children are a heritage of the Lord.

Helen and Rosalie Wert were here last night to see the babies, and they brought a big casserole for our dinner tomorrow. We're fortunate to have such good neighbors! Outside we're having another snowfall, a real, old-fashioned blizzard! Kermit had to go out into the swirling whiteness to help Chuck with the cattle, and when he came back in, he looked like a snowman. Oh well, before long the skies will clear and the sun will shine brilliantly on the dazzling splendor, making an exquisite sparkling display of the swirls, mounds, and sculptures the wind created. Julia had a dread of blizzards, but I like them, and I might as well, for we have our share of them. It's a typical scene here— wild, rugged, beautiful sights, and enough snow to gladden the heart of any snow-lover.

Kermit is on the rocker holding both babies and trying to get them to smile already. What a picture the three of them make! Sadie is baking cookies and singing as she works. What a blessing it is to have her as our helper!

Hannah and Henry are napping, so maybe I can take the time now to copy Aunt Miriam's poem. Then it's time to quit my ramblings and say "farewell."

Take Time with Your Children

Take time with your children,
For they are so dear—
They need your affection,
Your firm, loving care.
Take time to consider,
Their small joys and fears—
'Twill pay you in blessings,
Now and later in years.

Take time in the mornin,g
To greet them "Good day;"
To kiss them at bedtime,
And help them to pray.
An oft-given smile draws,
Their hearts close to you,
Give prayer example,
Their good keep in view.

Take time now to give them,
Correction they need—
Don't feel you're too busy,
Their errors to heed.
Delight it will give you,
To see them obey—
Neglect not this calling,
Take time, yes, today!

If one's hurt or troubled,
Take time to sit down,
And bind up their ouchie,
Or gladden the frown.
Their troubles are real,
Though small in our eyes,
Take heed lest their problems,
Your soul should despise.

Take time when they call you
To see a bright flower;
Take time to play with them—
'Twill brighten the hour.

Take time to wipe noses,
Or give them a drink,
Those seeds are quite small, but,
Important, I think.

Take time with them daily,
The Bible to read,
With prayer and with singing,
Their souls heavenward lead.
Their small minds are eager,
And ready to learn.
Oh, fill them with good thoughts,
To evil to spurn.

Take time in your prayer life,
God's guidance to ask;
Their care and their nurture—
It is a great task.
And then thank Him often,
For each dear one given;
Your lives were enriched by,
These jewels from Heaven.

Take time then, with Jesus,
The spirit to calm,
When they would seem naughty,
When work's going wrong.
A calm, cheerful parent,
Will go a long way,
In keeping them happy—
With joy end your day.

Take time to enjoy them,
For soon they'll be grown;
So learn from their lives, like,
A child to become.
Take time for their smiles and,
Their small, happy talk,
Rejoice in their blessings,
Like Christ daily walk.

- Author Unknown